The CHRISTMAS BOOK FLOOD

ROSEANNA M. WHITE

Tyndale House Publishers
Carol Stream, Illinois

Visit Tyndale online at tyndale.com.

Visit Roseanna M. White's website at roseannamwhite.com.

The Christmas Book Flood

Cover design by Sarah Susan Richardson

Edited by Kathryn S. Olson

Published in association with the literary agency of The Steve Laube Agency.

Library of Congress Cataloging-in-Publication Data

A catalog record for this book is available from the Library of Congress.

ISBN 979-8-4005-2743-2

Printed in the United States of America

32 31 30 29 28 27 26
7 6 5 4 3 2 1

Praise for Roseanna M. White

With her customarily reverent research, Roseanna M. White weaves a tale destined to reach deep into the hearts of word lovers everywhere. *The Christmas Book Flood* will be revisited by readers every Christmas . . . time and time again.

RACHEL MCMILLAN, bestselling author of *The Mozart Code*

With a strong baseline of little-known history, a sweet melody for Marcel and Zelie's building love, the rich harmony of Zelie's personal growth, and jarring notes of danger and betrayal, *The Spy Keeper of Marseille* thrills. Roseanna M. White has written another stellar World War II novel.

SARAH SUNDIN, bestselling, Christy Award–winning author of *Mists over the Channel Islands*

The Spy Keeper of Marseille captures the quiet ferocity of a woman and mother who lives out the dangerous beauty of doing what's right—even when it could cost her everything. Roseanna M. White delivers a story as brave as its heroine, proving that love and courage can change the course of history.

JANYRE TROMP, bestselling author of *Darkness Calls the Tiger*

Propulsively plotted and richly detailed. . . . A captivating historical romance and a resonant ode to the power of literature in dark times.

PUBLISHERS WEEKLY on *The Collector of Burned Books*

Brilliantly written. . . . [*The Collector of Burned Books*] captures the volatile intersection of art, academia, and authoritarian control, with the spark of unexpected romance bringing warmth to an unforgettable novel.

BOOKLIST starred review

ONE

REYKJAVIK, ICELAND
8 DECEMBER 1944

THE RINGING OF THE PHONE quite possibly kept Tatiana Eliasdottir from getting sacked. Its shrill cry brought her jumping to her feet, and a startled look at the clock on the wall showed her that had the phone not pulled her from the sentence half written on the paper in the typewriter, she would no doubt have been late to her job.

Frantic, she dashed for the telephone, silently thanking the Lord for whoever thought to call her so ridiculously early in the morning. Snatching the receiver from the cradle, she said, “Hello?” in a voice that probably sounded as breathless as she felt. She stretched the cord as far as it would go so she could reach the red jacket that matched her skirt. She’d draped it over a kitchen chair when she emerged from her bedroom an hour ago and made a mad dash for the typewriter, hoping to get down the idea she'd had before it flew away like a migratory bird.

"Oh good, you haven't left yet. I was afraid I'd missed you."

Tatiana's lips curled up at the voice on the line. She ought to have known, she supposed. Her sister was the only one who ever called first thing in the morning—something she'd only just been able to start doing six months ago, when phone lines were finally run to their rural hometown. "Ari! How are you feeling? How's Gunnar recuperating?"

Even across the miles, Ari's exhaustion came through loud and clear in her sigh. "That's why I'm calling. Gunnar reopened his wound yesterday, working."

With a wince, Tatiana cradled the phone between her head and shoulder so she could slide an arm into her jacket sleeve. Her brother-in-law had been on a fishing trawler that had been the unfortunate recipient of a German torpedo intended to attack an Allied shipping convoy. They'd been mistaken as part of it. The sailors had all survived, praise God—but several had been injured, including Gunnar. The doctor had ordered him to stay off his injured leg two weeks ago, but of course, this was Gunnar. He didn't understand the principle of *rest*. "How bad?"

"Bad enough that he's actually staying off his feet now." Ari's voice sounded strained. "And to make matters worse, the doctor ordered bed rest for me too."

Though she'd been reaching with an extended foot for her black pumps, Tatiana stopped at that, her hand tightening around the receiver. "Are you all right? The baby?" Her sister wasn't due to deliver until early January. And the last time the doctor had ordered bed rest, Ari had lost the child anyway, just a few weeks before she was supposed to give birth.

It couldn't happen again. It *couldn't*. Not now, so close to Christmas. Not now, when Ari had just finally, finally emerged from the fog of pain and grief of that late miscarriage two years ago, and the earlier ones three and four and five years ago. *Please, God. Please, spare my sister another loss. Please, keep the babe and her healthy.*

"I don't know." The crack in Ari's voice said far more than the words. "We're just . . . it's a hard time. And Elea—that's why I'm calling. With neither of us able to get up, it's going to be a miserable Christmas here for her. I'd hoped I might convince you to take a guest through the holidays."

"Truly?" A bubble of joy slipped past the concern keeping her throat in a death grip. Her seven-year-old niece was, quite possibly, her favorite person in the world. "You know I'd be delighted! But you really want to be separated at Christmas?"

"Of course I don't *want* to." Tears clogged her sister's voice. "But I think it would be best for her. You know how sensitive she is to everyone else's pain. She's as miserable as we are, and that's just not fair to her. She deserves a real celebration for once."

Tatiana finally slipped her feet into her shoes and glanced at the clock again. Two minutes until she had to be out the door. But the urgency didn't keep the sting of tears from her eyes. "You've done the best you could, Ari," she whispered into the phone. The series of miscarriages had wreaked havoc on her sister's soul. It was hard to think about Yule Lads and gifts and even the miracle of Jesus coming to earth as a babe when your heart was broken over the loss of your own babies. But she'd always tried to bring joy to her one living child. She deserved credit for that. "Elea doesn't begrudge anything."

"I know. That's why I so wanted this year to be different for her. And I know if she's with her favorite aunt, she'll have a festive holiday for once."

Tatiana smiled at the "favorite aunt" business. She was Elea's *only* aunt, given that she and Ari had no other siblings and Gunnar had only two younger brothers, neither of whom had married yet. "You know I'll gladly keep her. Perhaps she can even come with me to the office, and then to Uncle Valdi's for Christmas itself—she's always been so fascinated by the publishing company."

This marked the first Christmas since Tatiana moved to Reykjavik five years ago that she wouldn't go home for the holiday. She just couldn't get away, not this year. Not with the success of the Book Bulletin. It had been a heavy realization at first, but she'd cheered herself with the thought of spending more time with Valdi and his family. Having Elea here would make it even better.

"Thank you, Tatta. I feel so much better, knowing she'll have a cheerful holiday."

Another glance at the clock told her she needed to be out the door in five seconds. Hurriedly, she asked about how Elea would get to the city and promised to be home to meet the neighbor who'd be driving her on Monday afternoon. With a quick assurance that she'd call over the weekend to verify everything, Tatiana hung up the phone, grabbed her coat and hat and handbag, and dashed out the door with only one longing look at the half-finished sentence in her typewriter.

Stars twinkled overhead as she dashed out into the street, tugging her coat on as she went. Sunrise was still hours away, and they'd have less than four hours of daylight before night overtook them again. All of which she'd spend inside the proud brick facade that housed Sogufelagith—the Story Society. She probably wouldn't even get more than a fleeting glimpse of the sun through the window in her uncle's office, truth be told. Her own desk was in a windowless section outside his door, and the warehouse space in the basement where she'd likely be spending most of her time had nothing but electric lights.

But to get to work at one of Iceland's premier publishing houses, directly under her uncle, the publisher—it was worth the sacrifice of seeing any daylight this time of year. And really, she made up for it in the summer months, when day stretched on and on and nighttime was the one in short supply.

Uncle Valdi was a stickler for punctuality though, and had warned her from the start that she'd get no favoritism just because she was his brother's daughter. She'd seen him dismiss other people for late arrivals and didn't intend to be added to the list. So she ran the whole way to Fakafen, ignoring the snow that worked its way into her shoes when she misstepped and landed in a pile of it.

When she turned the corner onto the street that housed the publisher, the allure of a warm interior was enough to make her pick up her pace still more. "Hold the door, please!" she called out to whoever was entering before her.

The man paused and turned her way, giving her a glimpse of his face instead of just his fedora and wool coat in the light that spilled out of the open door. A face that, lately, had begun to make her chest go warm. She tried to act nonchalant whenever circumstances put her in the same place as the star of the Story Society, but to herself she could admit it was nothing but an act. When her uncle had offered her the position as his assistant, Anders Johannsson had been one of the reasons for her quick acceptance.

It wasn't the handsome face that now offered her a bashful smile, though that certainly didn't hurt—she hadn't known, then, how handsome he was. It wasn't the scads of books his editorial eye had helped bring to publication in his seven years at the company—though her uncle had bragged about his best editor on multiple occasions. It was his sagas that had intrigued her at the start, rewritten specifically for children and illustrated by his own hand. She'd always loved the old Icelandic tales of Nordic heroes of old, but the way he brought them to life was nothing short of brilliant. She'd purchased every single one he'd done thus far for Elea and already had his new release bought and wrapped for this year's gift.

She'd been quite certain she'd stumble and stutter the first time she met him . . . but was strangely comforted by the fact that the brilliant writer and illustrator was an absolute dunce in social situations. Hence how they'd gone years working together, and yet she hadn't begun to feel as though she knew him at all until these last few months.

The irony being he didn't know *she* was the one he'd been getting to know through letters. Thoughts she'd better stow away again now, lest she give herself away.

He paused in the doorway but couldn't seem to decide whether he should shut the door while he waited for her to dash the last few steps, thereby keeping the heat within the building, or hold it open for her. He half closed and then reopened it twice before she reached him, his cheeks flushing in that way they always did.

She couldn't have stopped her smile even had she wanted to. Which she assuredly didn't. Slipping in, she sent him the grin that Ari had always said could warm the heart of a snowman and waited for him to close the door behind himself. "Good morning, Anders."

He nodded, throat bobbing with a swallow. "Morning, Tatiana."

She wiped the snow from her shoes on the rug inside the door kept there for that purpose. "Are you excited for next week?"

He looked at her blankly. "Next week?"

A breath of laughter slipped out. "The official release of your new book."

"Ah." Why did his smile look so sad? They'd already had enough orders come in for it to guarantee it was as big a success as his last one—which was saying something. "Yes, of course. I always forget the actual day—given that I get my copies early."

As she had hers. Yet another perk of the position. She waited for him to join her before turning toward the stairs. "My niece is going to be ecstatic. They're her favorite books." She'd already told him as much each time she asked him to autograph them for her, but it bore repeating. In fact . . . "Oh! She's arriving in Reykjavik on Monday and will be coming into the office with me, assuming Uncle Valdi says it's all right. She'll be so excited to meet you."

At that, Anders's face relaxed a bit, his smile more genuine. "And I her. She's visiting before the holiday?"

"For it, actually." As they climbed up to the third floor where all the staff offices were, she gave him the short version of Gunnar's injury, Ari's bed rest, and their decision to ask for help. "I'm so excited to have her," she said as they reached the landing for their floor.

Anders grinned, pausing rather than turning immediately to his office on the right. "I imagine. And will the Yule Lads find her here?"

Tatiana's eyes went wide. She hadn't paused to consider that yet—but the Yule Lads would begin making their deposits of gifts in children's shoes the morning after Elea arrived. It was perfect timing . . . except that she had no gifts to sneak into her niece's footwear. "Well, I know what I'll be doing this weekend."

Anders watched Tatiana dash toward her small office attached to her uncle's large corner one, his lips refusing to give up their smile. He could admit that he'd been dubious at first, when he heard Valdi was hiring his niece to act as his assistant. In Anders's experience, working with family was as much a headache as it was a boon. But within a week, he'd had to recant his silent objections.

Tatiana was a spot of sunshine in the winter darkness. A trill of laughter in heavy silence. A scent of sugar and spice in a world of rations and lack.

He never dared say anything like that aloud, of course. If ever he tried, his tongue would tangle and his face would heat and his brothers' taunting would fill his mind. *Anders the Red-Faced Bookworm*, they'd called him as a lad. *Too backward for friends. You could bore a volcano to sleep.*

His fingers tightened around the handle of his briefcase, and he turned toward his own office door, since Tatiana had gone straight to her desk. It was different here at the Story Society, yes. These were his people. Other lovers of books, of the written word, of the storytelling that had undergirded Icelandic society for centuries. Here, he was understood. Appreciated. Lauded, even.

But it was hard to remember that after a visit from one of his family members, and it seemed one or another was dropping by his flat every other day. To ensure he was eating—his mother. To ask a favor—his little sister. To remind him of who he was and where he came from—all three of his elder brothers.

"Morning, Anders."

He looked up at the familiar voice of his assistant, Helga—who had quickly adopted Tatiana as her best friend upon the younger woman's hiring. Which of course meant Tatiana lingered outside his office, chatting with Helga, every spare moment, thereby distracting him constantly with her laughter and lyrical voice.

He smiled at the assistant who could still outwork anyone, even with gossip breaks factored in. "Morning, Helga."

"I put the post on your desk. There were several you've been waiting for." She named several of the authors he'd been working with, all of which made him nod.

"Perfect. Thank you." There was nothing like attending to his correspondence to get his mind back into publishing and away from home.

Last night both Mother and his eldest brother, Dalmar, had dropped in after the fishing boats had returned to Reykjavik harbor for the day. Their mother had fussed over his largely bare cupboards, as always, and put a pot of fish stew she'd brought for him on the stove to heat. "From yesterday's catch," she'd said, sending him that look of disapproval as pointed as an icicle. "You should thank your brothers for providing for you."

Twelve years since he'd left the life of a fisherman and pursued higher education. Seven since he'd landed the job at the

Story Society. One would think that would have been time enough to grow a few calluses when it came to his family. But each jab hurt anew.

He knew his lines in the script of their lives, though. He'd nodded to Dalmar, head of their family's trawler since Father had passed away six years ago. "Thank you, Dalmar. Though you didn't have to bring me food. I was going to the grocer's after I put away my work." Though he knew it was useless, he pulled his wallet from his pocket. "Please, allow me to pay—"

"Don't insult your brother." Mother had frowned and pointed the wooden spoon at him, spattering a few drops of stew on the floor. "You are still part of this family. We take care of our own."

Yet they refused to allow him to use his salary to help with repairs to the boat. Fishing could support itself, they always said. Especially now that they were exporting their catches to America—one of many benefits to find them since the Americans had occupied their country.

Part of him couldn't help but think they refused, though, so that they had something to hold over him—all the fish they brought him, despite the fact that he never asked for any of it, was a debt he then owed. Never mind that he didn't need it, never mind that he brought in more money through his editing work and his books than they did put together from fishing. In his family's eyes, he was nothing but a pretender. Stories, they'd always said, might be what made an evening bright as they gathered around the fire, but they weren't something to make a living from.

He set his briefcase on his desk and shucked off his coat, scarf, and hat, praying for the millionth time that the Lord would give him armor to protect him from those opinions. He knew he was following the call of God by dedicating his life to words instead of fishing. He'd never for a moment doubted it. But somehow, knowing it didn't make his family's disapproval hurt any less.

Coffee. He needed coffee to help dislodge the fog of stress from his brain, and he hadn't had any at home. He'd meant to pick some up from the grocer's last night but had ended up not going, since his mother had provided dinner and then lingered, telling tales of his nieces and nephews, until after the store would have been closed.

The coffeepot was a relatively new addition to the office, but a popular one. He could have asked Helga to fetch him a cup, but she was already on the telephone, so he opted to go himself rather than wait. A crowd of his colleagues were already queued up, waiting for their turn, chatting amongst themselves. Anders took his place at the back of the gaggle, wondering not for the first time how they could be so fortunate.

The other Nordic countries were occupied too—but by the Nazis. There, they knew from the few Icelanders who had managed to come home after being trapped in Denmark or Sweden, private citizens were starving and dying of cold, because the Germans took it all. All their resources, all their livelihoods. The people were left with nothing.

Here, it was the opposite. The Americans had brought prosperity with them. Money they were eager to spend in

Icelandic shops, for starters. Then they opened exports of fish, bringing another influx of cash, and that trickled down to everyone. For the first time in their history, he and his neighbors not only had enough, they had *extra*. Industry was booming. Cities and towns were growing. They'd gone from being the poorest country in Europe to one of the wealthiest, per capita.

It was a humbling thing, to be benefiting from the war that had been tearing so much of the world apart.

"I don't know, Tatta." Valdi's voice snagged Anders's attention, drawing his gaze to the publisher's door, which stood open, displaying both the middle-aged man and his beautiful niece on opposite sides of his wide wooden desk. "Things are going to be hectic between now and Christmas. Having a child underfoot . . ."

A hole cleared in front of the coffeepot, but Anders edged forward only a few inches. None of his business, he knew that. But he couldn't help but feel a little invested. Tatiana's face always lit up so when she was speaking of her niece. He often asked about little Elea, just to see the way her eyes would go bright.

Surely Valdi wouldn't deny his grandniece the company of family in the days before Christmas. Would he?

Tatiana's back was to the door, but he could see the plea in the line of her shoulders, even before he heard it in her voice when next she spoke. "You know Elea won't be any trouble though. She'll stay at my desk and occupy herself with books or drawings or the schoolwork she'll be bringing with her, since she's missing the last ten days of class. I promise, you'll scarcely know she's here, but for the smiles she'll inspire."

Valdi's lips were pressed together, his eyes declaring himself conflicted. "You know I want to help—but if you leave her at your desk while you're overseeing the mailings, then she'll be unchaperoned unless I put aside my work to watch her."

"Helga and I could help." The words were out of Anders's mouth before he could think better of declaring to his boss that he'd been unabashedly eavesdropping. And his feet, fools that they were, were propelling him toward the open door. All for exactly what he'd been hoping—Tatiana spinning around, beaming a smile of gratitude at him.

Fool, without question. He knew very well that nothing would ever convince a woman like Tatiana to give him a second glance. He had only to stand beside his hulking older brothers with their strapping good looks to be reminded of all he wasn't. Dalmar and Ulric and Ram had always had girls swooning—and had all been married for years at this point. He, on the other hand, could never keep a woman's attention for more than five minutes.

Still, he could never help himself when it came to Tatiana. She was never stingy with her smiles and gave them to everyone, it was true, but he lived for the ones directed his way. Like the one currently cutting through the clouds like a ray of sunshine.

Her uncle, on the other hand, lifted his brows. "You think you or Helga will have time for babysitting, Anders?"

"I'm a few days ahead of schedule on the manuscript I'm editing. And there's plenty of room for her in my outer office with Helga—and you know how she loves children, and she can outpace the rest of the Story Society anyway. She wouldn't be a bother." He offered a smile of his own. "And perhaps she'll do me the favor of looking over my own work in progress. I could use the feedback of a few children and haven't had the chance to show it to my own nieces and nephews yet."

Because when he'd tried after dinner with the whole clan on Sunday, Ulric had told him to put his rubbish away so the children could go outside to play.

Tatiana drew in a happy gasp, hands clasped together before her heart. "Truly? She will be over the moon! Elea adores Helga."

He let her pleasure warm him for a moment before looking past her to see what Valdi's reaction might be.

Thankfully, the publisher was smiling too, though with a few more reservations in his eyes. "All right. We'll give it a try. But if it doesn't work out, she'll have to stay with Beta during the days instead. Fair enough?"

Having met Valdi's wife many times, he had no doubt she'd be eager to host little Elea if it came to that. But taking her to her aunt and uncle's house and then picking her up again would steal the moments he knew Tatiana was hoping to spend with her niece.

She moved her smile from Anders to her uncle and back again. "Thank you. Both of you. You won't regret it—I promise."

Elea could be a little monster, and he still wouldn't regret it. Anything that earned him that smile was something he'd do gladly. Feeling his face begin to heat in that way he hated, he merely nodded and ducked back into the coffee line.

TWO

11 DECEMBER 1944

Darkness had long ago fallen, bringing with it a biting cold wind off the water. That wasn't enough to keep Tatiana inside though, not with the promise of her niece's arrival any minute. She'd hurried home from work, changed from her stylish pumps into sturdy snow boots and a longer woolen skirt than she'd worn to the office, and come back outside to wait.

She stood in a circle of light from the streetlamp, grateful that the Americans had never succeeded in instituting the blackouts they'd at first demanded. The mayor had kept putting them off, insisting the threat to Iceland by the Luftwaffe was minimal, and it had proven true enough that their occupiers had let the subject drop. Tatiana paced around the circle of light, trying to keep her feet from going numb in the cold.

"Evening, Tatta," her neighbor, Ofelia, said as she approached the entrance to their building. Her arms were full of grocery bags, so Tatiana leapt for the door to hold it for her.

"Hello, Ofelia." Though her face was freezing, she had no trouble offering a smile for the woman who had adopted her as another granddaughter within a week of her moving in. "Find what you needed at the grocer's?"

Ofelia made a face, sending a beautiful web of wrinkles fanning out from her eyes. "At this rate I'll only have sugar enough for a batch or two of Christmas treats. And I've been saving it up so long!"

Tatiana had been saving her rations too, intending to give them to either Ofelia or Aunt Beta to use in their holiday baking . . . but that was before she knew Elea would be here. Now she was planning to bake some treats herself, and since she hadn't ever mentioned her intentions to her neighbor or aunt . . . well, they'd understand, regardless. "I know. I've made a list of Elea's favorites, and I'll let her pick which two or three we can make."

"Sometimes I wonder if there will ever be a day when the rationing stops." Ofelia smiled though as she lingered in the doorway, gaze on Tatiana. "Not that we have anything to complain about. There's still fresh milk, potatoes, fish . . ."

"And paper," Tatiana added with a grin of her own. Paper had never been rationed at all, which made books one of the few readily available luxuries. And now that people had extra money to spend on them . . . well, business was booming at the Story Society.

Her neighbor chuckled and stepped inside. "Indeed. I can't wait for my order from the Book Bulletin to arrive."

"Soon," Tatiana could promise. She knew that the other publishers in Reykjavik were working as hard as her own was to get all those orders processed and shipped out to arrive in time for Christmas.

Easier said than done, given the number of orders still pouring in. The response to Iceland's first joint-effort book catalogue, which the country's publishing companies had decided to put out this year to celebrate their new independence from Denmark, had exceeded all their expectations. The catalogue had gone to every household in Iceland—an investment that was a gamble for the companies. But Valdi had said today after a meeting with the other publishers that they were all showing more profits for the season than in the past three years combined, and there were still two weeks left for orders to come in. The Book Bulletin was a smashing success.

Her blood still buzzed a bit when she thought of it. Thought of all those books soon to arrive in all those homes. Of all the hands that would receive them, wrap them, give them. Of all the faces that would be limned with delight when they tore away those wrappings and saw the hours of joy waiting inside each cover.

Apparently her continued awe at being part of such a miracle was on her face, given the way Ofelia laughed and reached out to pat her cheek with a mittened hand. "Sweet Tatta. Bring Elea round when you have the time. I'm eager to see how big she's grown."

"I will." She shut the door behind her neighbor and turned back to the street when the rumble of a lorry's engine broke the relative quiet of the star-studded evening. The streetlights glinted off the dented, rusting vehicle, making her grin anew. Lambi Larsson had been driving that same lorry for over a decade already and would be driving it still until it fell apart, she had no doubt.

She waved as it squealed to a halt, dashing into the street to open the passenger-side door. "Elea!"

Her niece turned toward her, but no smile turned her lips. No laughter bubbled forth. No little arms flew around her. Instead, a quiet "Hey, Aunt Tatta" slipped out as Elea slid off the bench seat and to the ground.

Tatiana's brows pinched together, and she sent a questioning look to Lambi. Her old neighbor, her father's childhood best friend, sighed. "It was a quiet trip," he said, reaching for the handle of the small suitcase sitting on the seat between them. "I'll take this up for you."

"Thanks. There's dinner and coffee ready, if you're hungry, Lambi." With a hand on Elea's shoulder, she led her off the street and toward her building.

Lambi waved that away. "Kind of you, but I need to get to my cousin's."

She nodded, not minding that she'd be left alone with her niece sooner rather than later. Elea's small, gloved fingers found their usual place in her hand as they moved into the building and up the stairs. "We're going to have so much fun," Tatiana promised as they climbed. "I'll tell you all my ideas as we eat, and you can decide what all we'll do."

Elea gave a slow, disinterested nod, making Tatiana press her lips together. It was no surprise that her niece was sad to be away from her parents for Christmas. Even so, this was the first time in years she'd not been greeted with an enthusiastic hug.

She'd left the door to her flat unlocked and soon had it open so that Lambi could bring the suitcase in. He left again with a warm farewell and a *"Glethileg jol!"*

Tatiana returned the "Merry Christmas" and closed the door behind him. Pivoting back to Elea, who still stood just inside the door, she clapped her hands together. "Well. Let's get our coats and boots off and eat. Are you hungry?"

Elea's only answer was a shrug as she reached for her buttons.

Emotions—hope and fear and so many others—twisted up inside Tatiana as she toed off her own boots and hung her coat on the rack by the door. Elea was sometimes quiet, but never before had she seen her so sullen. After she'd put away all their winter things, she crouched down before her niece and clasped her shoulders. "Are you all right, *hugljuf*?"

She often called her niece "sweet one," but when tears gathered in Elea's eyes, Tatiana silently berated herself for the choice—it was what Ari always called her too. She ought to have chosen a different endearment. Afraid to say anything else and make it worse, she opted for pulling Elea into a tight embrace.

There. Little arms came around her and held on tight, and a moment later, a sob caught in Elea's throat.

It brought answering tears to Tatiana's eyes. She pulled them over to the sofa without letting go and sat, Elea climbing into her lap. Soon, she'd be too big for such a position, but just now, it was what they both needed. Tatiana wrapped her arms around the little one and rocked back and forth with her.

Many minutes later, Elea's cries quieted to gasps for breath. Tatiana rubbed a hand lightly over her back in the way she'd always liked. "There now," she whispered. "It's going to be all right."

Elea buried her face in Tatiana's chest. "Sorry," she managed between shaking breaths.

"You don't need to apologize." She pressed a kiss to the top of her niece's blonde head. "I know this isn't easy, being away from home for Christmas. But we're going to have a wonderful time, you and I. You'll see. You're going to come to the office with me, and do you know who has a little desk set up for you in his outer office? Anders Johannsson! You'll be right beside Helga."

Elea didn't lift her face. "Why not in *your* office?"

Her laugh came out a bit forced. "Because I'll be spending far too many hours in the warehouse, overseeing all the orders from the Book Bulletin. Did you see it? Our catalogue? Did you pick out any books you want?"

Never one to be distracted by shiny things, Elea finally leaned back enough to meet Tatiana's gaze—her own far harder than a seven-year-old's should be. "You won't even be there?"

Bother. Anders's and Helga's company was supposed to be a treat, not a sentence. "The warehouse is in the basement, so I won't be far. And if you'd rather come down with me, that's fine too." She had no idea if it was or not, actually—she hadn't thought to ask Uncle Valdi if that would be possible. But if her uncle disapproved, he would at least take it up privately with Tatiana and not say something in front of Elea, she knew. "Or if you'd rather, you could visit Grandaunt Beta during the days."

The quiver of Elea's lips said she did *not* rather.

All right then. The office it was. "Do you know what else we have in our common room? Shelves full of all the books we've published. There's an entire bookcase full of children's books, and you'll be able to read any you like." *That* she knew Uncle Valdi would approve. He'd in fact said to pay attention to which ones she favored, and he'd give them to her for Christmas.

Elea sniffed and wiped at her cheeks. "*Sagas for Children*? Mamma wouldn't let me bring mine. She said they took up too much room."

Anders would be touched to know she'd wanted to. Tatiana gave a solemn nod. "Of course! We have all of Anders Johannsson's books on display—and he said he needs a little girl to read his next book and look at his drawings . . . if you're willing."

Finally, finally a hint of the true Elea. Her eyes went wide, a mix of delight and incredulity swirling in their blue-gray depths. "Me? Read one that isn't published yet?"

"Mm-hmm. He usually has his nieces and nephews read them first, but they haven't had the chance yet. He said your thoughts would be invaluable." Unable to stop herself, she reached up and smoothed back the pale golden locks sticking to the tear tracks on her niece's cheeks, tucking them behind her ears. When Elea's stomach rumbled, Tatiana smiled. "Sounds like someone *is* hungry. I have *kjotsupa* ready, and some rye bread." She knew Elea loved their family's recipe for lamb soup.

First, though, a visit to the bathroom to wash the tears from her cheeks and see to her needs. While Elea took a few minutes to gather herself, Tatiana busied herself in her tiny kitchen, setting two bowls and plates on the table and pouring glasses of milk to drink. By the time her guest reappeared, everything was ready, and a Christmas song had found its way to her lips.

Just as a prayer had found its way to her heart. *Help me be what she needs, Lord God. Help me give her a good Christmas.*

Elea climbed onto the chair she always used whenever she visited, her gaze darting to the darkened bedroom. "Did you make me my bed on the floor again?"

Tatiana smiled. "Of course. And I used *six* blankets for your mattress."

At long last, a small smile peeked out from the storm clouds. "Last time it was only five."

"Ah, but I got a new one for my birthday. It's the top layer. Still, if it's too cold on the floor—"

"I can sleep on the sofa. I know. But I'll be fine." Elea rested her hand on the table, palm up.

Another cause to smile. Not every family held hands while they prayed a blessing for the food, but theirs did. Tatiana settled her hand over Elea's and said a short prayer, thanking God not only for the food but for Elea's safe arrival and for the time to spend together.

Elea took a few spoonfuls of her soup before she said, "My friends are all jealous that I get to miss school. And come here. Rafney thinks you're so glamorous."

Tatiana laughed around her soup. "I would have thought so too, when I was your age. But sadly, there is little glamour. Still, I love living here and working for the Story Society. Perhaps you can take a book home for Rafney."

They talked about school and Elea's friends while they ate, which seemed a safer subject than all the plans Tatiana had made for the visit. There would be time enough to decide on those once Elea had better adjusted to being here. Once they were finished, she suggested Elea call her mother while Tatiana cleaned up. She helped her dial and waited to make sure Ari picked up before moving to store the leftovers and do the dishes. Still, she couldn't help but keep an ear attuned to the conversation.

Not that Elea said much more than yes and no. The call was short, but when Elea hung up, she was sniffling again and running for the bathroom.

Tatiana sighed and scrubbed her soup pot with renewed vigor. She'd thought talking to her mother would help, but perhaps it would be better if they limited the telephone calls home.

She'd finished up the dishes by the time Elea emerged again, once more silent and drooping as she shuffled toward the sofa. Tatiana dried her hands, hung the towel, and decided to try for cheer again. "Don't forget to put a shoe in the window tonight. Stekkjastaur is coming."

Elea sent her a positively withering glare. "Aunt Tatta. I am *far* too old to believe in the Yule Lads."

Tatiana planted her hands on her hips. "What nonsense is this? *I* still believe in the Yule Lads!"

Her niece rolled her eyes, though she thought she detected a hint of a smile trying to worm its way to the corners of her mouth. "You do not."

"Of course I do. They're as much a part of Christmas as leaf bread and ginger cookies. They help us remember why we celebrate, the miracle of Jesus leaving his home in heaven for us." To prove it, she bustled over to the entryway where their winter gear waited and plucked two shoes—one of Elea's and one of her own—from the floor. She carried both into the living room and set them on the floor in front of Elea. "We'll both put one in the windowsill. So when Stekkjastaur comes, he has a place to leave his presents. Don't let me forget to put milk out for him. I'm afraid I haven't any cookies yet, but I think he'll forgive it, given the rationing."

Elea let out a blustery sigh far too old for her age. "Aunt Tatta, I know you're trying to be nice, but . . . but I know they're not *real*. You don't have to pretend."

"Not real?" It wasn't the calling out of myths as such that made her pause. That made her dig in. It was the utter dejection underscoring her niece's words. The despair in her tone. Tatiana sat beside her on the sofa. "What makes a story real, anyway? It isn't about whether there's really a witch named Gryla who gobbles up naughty children." She made claws of her hands and used them to tickle Elea until she shrieked with laughter. Tatiana grinned. "It isn't about whether Gryla truly has thirteen trolls for sons who hike down from their mountain caves to visit children before Christmas. You know that, don't you? The stories are about what they mean to us. What they teach us. Just like the sagas you love."

Elea fidgeted with one of the buttons on her dress. "The sagas are ancient. No one tries to pretend they really happened that way, with magic and everything. No one tries to tell us we have to believe them. But the Yule Lads?" She looked up, something dark and glinting in her eyes. "If they're real, then they're awfully forgetful. Last year only three of them remembered me." The glint turned to tears, but she blinked them furiously away.

Tatiana had to as well. She'd known Ari had been in bad shape emotionally last Christmas. But had she really only remembered to put a gift in her daughter's shoe three times, instead of the traditional thirteen? It made her heart break, not just for Elea, but for Ari too. How deep must her sister's despair have reached, to eclipse what had once been the greatest joy of their own childhoods?

Ari had *loved* the Yule Lads. The utter ridiculousness of them, how they combined the silly with the scary. Presents and pranks. How often had they jested with each other about the danger of receiving rotten potatoes instead of sweets or gifts if they got caught being naughty?

She reached out and brushed her fingertips over the satin-soft skin of Elea's cheek. "Of course they're forgetful sometimes. They live hard lives in the mountains, with nothing but rocks and snow for company. And they're old, you know. It takes some of them days to make their way down. They get tired now and then and don't make it all the way to each home."

Elea looked away, lips quivering a bit again. "I know she tries," she said in a whisper so quiet Tatiana scarcely heard it. "I know how it hurt her to lose the babies. But she still has *me*. Why . . . why am I not enough? Why can't she remember that I'm *here*?"

"Oh, precious." Tatiana slid an arm around her and pulled her to her side. "She loves you more than life itself. She knows you're here."

"But I'm *not*!" The words ended on a cry that was more shout than tears, and she pulled free of Tatiana's arms. "She sent me away—for *Christmas*."

How to make a seven-year-old understand, when Tatiana wasn't sure she did herself? She couldn't know what Ari felt, not really. She'd never lived through those losses in the same way. She didn't have to battle that black cloud every day. All she knew was that her sister loved this little girl wholly, and that everything she did was for her good. "Because she knows how the Yule Lads failed you last year, Elea." She spoke softly to counteract her niece's shout. "She knows that a little girl as wonderful as you should have gotten treat upon treat in her shoes. And she wanted to make sure that this year, things were different."

Elea was a clever girl. Yes, she knew that it was her parents who gave the gifts—but that didn't mean she didn't still want them. The stories, the treats, the laughter—the assurance that she was loved. Her fingers curled into the fabric of her dress, her nostrils flaring.

Tatiana leaned closer, until their arms were touching. "You know that Stekkjastaur is the eldest of the thirteen brothers, don't you? He's been traveling for days already, to get here in time. If you listen, you can hear the creaking of his old knees." She paused, making a show of listening. When a creak sounded from above, even Elea grinned. Of course they both knew it was the neighbor in the flat above them. But that wasn't the point. "When your mother and I were growing up on the farm, we would make certain the sheep were all safe in the barn on the eleventh of December. Because that sneaky Stekkjastaur would steal the very milk from the mother ewes if we let him. That's why we always set out a glass of milk for him—so he wouldn't bother the sheep."

Elea shook her head, but a bit of light had reentered her eyes. "You don't have any sheep in Reykjavik."

"All the more reason to set out the milk. Think how thirsty he must be after his long travels!" Tatiana winked. "I always liked Stekkjastaur. He's kind and clever, you know. Though stubborn too. 'Like two little girls I know,' my father used to say."

Elea's smile faded again. "My *pabbi*'s leg is hurting him so much. I could have helped. I wouldn't have been trouble—I'd have *helped*."

"They know that." Another stroke over her silky hair. "That's exactly why they asked if you could visit me instead. They know you'd spend your entire Christmas helping *them*. When what they wanted was to give *you* something." She rested her cheek against Elea's head. "I know I'm not your mamma or *pabbi*, Elea. But I love you so much. And I am so, so glad you're here with me. I was upset about not getting to go home for Christmas this year. But now? I think it'll be the best holiday I've had in ages."

Elea heaved another monstrous sigh. But then she pushed off the couch, bent to pick up the two shoes, and strode to the window with determined steps to set them both on the sill.

It was victory enough for this evening.

Tired from the trip and the emotions, Elea didn't ask to stay up late. In fact, it was before her usual bedtime that she started her preparations and cuddled into the nest of blankets Tatiana had made for her—just like the beds their grandmother had made for her and Ari whenever they spent the night at their grandparents' house as children. They prayed together, and Tatiana pressed a kiss to Elea's forehead before padding back out of her bedroom, pulling the door shut all but a few inches.

Her gaze tracked to her typewriter, but despite the itching in her fingers to press them to the keys, she wasn't about to create such a clatter before her niece had a chance to fall asleep. So instead, she sat at her desk but opened the drawer that held the pages already written and pulled out the last several chapters.

She had no idea if it was any good. But then, she hadn't known if her previous attempts were worthwhile either. It had taken a saga-worthy amount of courage to put the manuscript in the post for the Story Society eighteen months ago, submitted under a pseudonym. She'd been sick to her stomach when she'd seen first Anders and then her uncle reading it, neither having a clue she was the author.

They still didn't know, even though they'd offered a contract. Even though they'd gone through the editorial process, all by post. Even though the first copies had come into the warehouse three weeks ago, and she'd had to pretend like her heart wasn't racing like a runaway sleigh. She'd chosen a masculine pen name—because while women were finally beginning to break into the publishing world in Iceland, it seemed the only books being published by them were all about women defying the patriarchal expectations put upon them.

Not that Tatiana disagreed with their stances, per se . . . but those weren't the stories she wanted to write. Her mind was filled always with tales of adventure and mystery, a dash of romance thrown in. Not quite sagas, like the ones Anders so masterfully retold for children. But not dissimilar in some of the themes.

She'd known she couldn't submit her work under her own name. Not to the Story Society, because of the bias—either positive or negative—that came of being the publisher's niece. But not to any other publisher either, because they would take one look at the feminine ending of her name and put her into a predetermined slot of expectations. So the story she'd written and rewritten and edited and now could, amazingly, hold in her hands was under the name of Tandri Ebbisson—both more distant family names.

She'd asked for only ten copies to be provided to her, because she knew she'd never be able to explain away a whole case of them. One was now on her shelf, alphabetized in the rest of her fiction collection. The others she had stashed away under her bed, intending to give them as gifts. It wouldn't look odd—she *always* gave books as gifts to her family and friends, especially in the last several years, when nothing else was readily available.

Though she'd debated confessing her authorship to Ari, she hadn't yet. Wasn't sure she ever would, honestly. Every time she considered it, her stomach went tight and sour.

What if everyone hated the book? Or what if this next one underway even now in her typewriter was as horrible as she feared it would be? She was enjoying the writing of it and thought it was as good as her debut . . . but she couldn't be certain. Anders had, after all, pointed out plot holes and mistakes in her first book that she'd completely missed. Thereby proving yet again how brilliant he was.

She'd found herself gazing at him far too often in the

last year, wondering how that mind of his did all it did. Wondering how he could hide such deep thoughts under a perfectly calm, even bashful exterior. Wondering at the fact that she felt as though she were getting to know him so much through the notes he sent to her postbox with thoughts on her story, becoming truly friends and not just colleagues . . . yet he had no idea that *she* was the Tandri with whom he'd struck up such a rapport. More than once she'd considered telling *him*, too. But she didn't dare.

Once she'd reread her chapters, a quick check at the bedroom door told her Elea was sound asleep, so she settled back at the typewriter, knowing her niece could sleep through anything once she was out. She wrote for an hour, until her own exhaustion said she'd better stop.

She drank the glass of milk they'd set out for Stekkjastaur, slipped some of the coveted chocolate she'd found into the two shoes in the windowsill . . . and paused for a long moment to look out into the shadow-deep night. Green and pink streaked the sky near the horizon that stretched out over the harbor, stalling her as effectively as a hand reached out to hers.

Another reason she didn't mind the long nights this time of year. How could she, when they provided such an endless canvas for some of the Lord's most beautiful paintings? She watched the aurora dance for many long minutes, until the chill seeping through the pane of glass chased her away.

But even the cold, even the memory of her niece's tears couldn't erase the peace the colors had painted on her soul.

The Lord was master of them all, their lives another of his canvases. And in this season designed to remind them of the greatest expression of his love, she would pray his light danced over every part of them. And trust it would be exactly what he intended.

THREE

12 DECEMBER 1944

Tatiana checked her watch and dashed back over to the warehouse space for another box of *Sagas for Children*. She was running behind for the day already, through no fault of her own. The orders she'd been filling had more books in them than the ones she'd done thus far, which meant more time was required to fill each one.

A good problem. But still a problem. She and the regular mail room workers had done their best to organize everything, but they were all running about today with mounting panic. Her own redoubled as she stopped in front of the spot suspiciously empty of boxes. "No. Where are the newest sagas?" She directed the question to the nearest mail room worker.

Bjarni shook his head. "Out. I sent Jon to the warehouse for more, and of Tandri's too. Ran out of both half an hour ago."

Tatiana's scalp prickled. Hers? Her book had enough orders that they'd run out of the supply here too? She'd seen the pile of boxes that had been delivered a week ago, she knew how many were in each one. That they'd needed more of Anders's titles was no surprise, but he was a known quantity. She—or her pen name, anyway—was not.

"Post is here," someone shouted from the front of the room.

Tatiana scurried back out of the cave of boxes. When the first orders had begun to arrive, she'd scarcely believed that the idea Valdi had run by her back in the summer was actually coming to fruition. She'd been the one to suggest the method of fulfillment all the companies had decided on, so she'd taken responsibility for the logistics of it as well. Each Book Bulletin had order forms for each of the companies represented inside it, so they were each responsible for filling only their own titles. She knew that Valdi and the other publishers had considered shipping books to a central warehouse and hiring someone to fill *all* the orders, but without knowing what the response would be, it had seemed an unnecessary risk and expense. Easier by far was to create multiple forms for inclusion.

And to see their dream working? Orders coming in daily? That was enough to make her push aside how far behind she already was today and hurry to see how many more forms she'd need to process this afternoon.

But she paused when she caught the look on the postman's face. He held a large canvas sack, which was nothing out of the ordinary—he usually gave her a smile and reached inside for the portion of it that was for the Story Society. Today, however, he lifted his brows and set the whole bag down.

Tatiana followed its descent with her gaze. "It's not . . . all of that, is it?"

The postman huffed. "And more besides. I'll bring the other one in next."

No. He must be joking. Or perhaps someone had made a mistake and put some of the other publishers' forms into the bag for them. She darted forward and unzipped the bag, fully expecting to pull out a handful of envelopes addressed to another company.

But no. All the same, and all correct. All to *them*. Dozens . . . scores . . . hundreds of forms. For a moment, just one, excitement still surged through her. Never in her wildest dreams had she imagined the Bulletin would be such a success!

Then reality crashed in. Christmas was thirteen days away, and not all of those could be used for mailing out orders, which of course had to arrive *before* that holy day. That meant that she had, what, a week? A week to get all of these orders sorted, filled, boxed, weighed, and put back into the hands of the postal service?

She lifted her head, her gaze clashing with Bjarni's. He stood there on the other side of the little table she'd been using for her work, mouth agape and panic in his eyes that surely matched hers. "There's . . ." *No way.* There was no way they could get through all of these orders in such a short amount of time, just the four of them. Especially since Jon would no doubt be constantly driving between here and the warehouse to try to keep their books in stock. There just wasn't enough room here to store all the ones they'd need.

Bjarni scrubbed a hand over his face. "Never once occurred to me that this could be *too* successful. What do we do, Tatta?"

The postman brought in the second bag, but rather than set this one down, he unzipped it. Tatiana drew in a breath, hoping that meant he'd just take out a twine-wrapped section, like he usually did.

But no. He poured them all out onto the table, shaking the stragglers loose. Then reached for the first bag and did the same, mumbling something about needing the canvas sacks back.

The mountain of envelopes turned into an avalanche, spilling off the table and into Tatiana's lap as the postman pivoted and left again with a call of "Good luck."

Her eyes stung. Her nose clogged. Her throat went tight.

She'd have to spend every waking hour in this mail room, and still she wouldn't get finished in time. And Elea! Her niece was here so that she could have a *good* holiday, so that she could receive the attention she deserved. Not so that she could be ignored while her guardian feverishly shoved books into boxes.

Elea would never want to visit her again. Ari would scream at Tatiana for neglecting the child so desperate for the attention of an adult who loved her. And when she failed to get all these orders out on time—which she would—Valdi would sack her. Maybe all of them.

No. No, she had to protect the regular mail room workers. This wasn't their fault. She was the one who'd promised her uncle she could take care of the extra load. She'd been the one to suggest to him that each company should fill its own orders rather than renting a warehouse and hiring all new staff. This was her problem. Her mess. Her doing.

Her *un*doing.

Try as she might to hold it all together, the tears overcame her resolve and leaked out onto her cheeks. She dashed them away, tried to regulate her breathing, tried to tilt her face down so no one else would see how ridiculous she was being, but it was all too much.

This was supposed to be a celebration, this entire enterprise. A celebration of Iceland, newly independent. Of a nation somehow flourishing despite this horrible war. Of the stories they were known for, that they were producing in record numbers.

This was supposed to be a visit that her niece would remember with joy and laughter.

This was supposed to be a happy secret Tatiana could smile over to herself, as she packed up hundreds of copies of her own books and prayed over each one, that its recipient would find what they needed in the pages, something to touch their hearts and inspire them.

She heard Jon return and caught Bjarni mumbling something to him about fetching Valdi. That was enough to convince her to shove the envelopes off her legs, to push herself to her feet.

The situation didn't look any better from the added height. Worse, if anything. Now she could see the full chaos on the table.

She wiped her cheeks again, though more tears took the place of the ones she dashed away.

Bjarni, who'd been working at the Story Society longer even than Uncle Valdi, patted her shoulder. "I don't blame you for the tears, Tatta. Frankly, I agree. This is too much. It's hopeless, unless your uncle hires an army to help us. We'll never get through them all."

"And more could still come tomorrow." Her shoulders sagged, and she couldn't blame it on the added weight of Bjarni's hand. "What happens to the ones we can't fill in time? Do we send them out late? Refund them?"

Usually the old-timer was full of smiles and optimism. Usually, he'd have said, *Don't you worry, Tatta, we'll get them all out.* Today, he just sighed and shook his head. "I don't know."

Though she knew she ought to get started—open all the envelopes, set the checks in a pile to be taken to the bank, make a list of all the books in the orders so they could try to get enough here from the warehouse—she couldn't bring herself to slit open even one. Once she started, she'd be chained to this table for the foreseeable future.

More of the stupid tears welled.

She heard her uncle's footsteps as he approached, heard his sharp intake of breath when he spotted Mount Envelope. He came up on Tatiana's other side and let out a low whistle. "All of these came today? And they're all for us?"

A nod was all she could manage.

Bjarni spoke up. "That's more in one day than everything we've gotten up until now combined." He gave her shoulder one last squeeze and dropped his hand. "No way we can handle this, boss. Not the four of us in the time we have, even though Tatiana's an organizational whiz."

Was she? She'd been pretty proud of her system up until now, but this inundation quickly overwhelmed her careful dikes.

Silence pulsed for several heartbeats. Then Valdi motioned with a hand, catching Jon's eye. "Bring the carts. Let's load them up with as many of these as they'll hold."

Tatiana's brows drew together. "Why?"

Her uncle's smile was just as it always was—calm, wise, gentle, but firm. "Because we need to make an appeal to the staff, and I think a visual will help us. We need volunteers, as many of them as we can get. If we have to push back editorial deadlines by a week, then we'll do it. This takes precedence."

She could only blink. Never, in her five years at the Story Society, had her uncle ever prioritized anything above the editorial and publication schedule. It was the heart and soul of the company, he'd always said. Anyone could learn the mail room—though Bjarni had been running it with particular skill for decades. Editors were another case entirely. "You're going to pull editorial staff down here?"

"The ones who volunteer. And tell them to recruit family members too." Her uncle reached out and grabbed a handful of envelopes. All identical in size, in shape, but inside, all would be unique. "These aren't just orders for books. They're how our people will celebrate Christmas this year. They're the stories through which we'll remember the coming of Jesus. They're gifts, carefully chosen by people who have little other options for things to give as long as the war is raging. And we . . ." He turned back to her, to Bjarni, and grinned. "We all get to play St. Nicholas, as the Americans would say. Yule Lads. We get to deliver these gifts to each family so that they can brighten someone's life with a story. That's not just a noble call—it's a sacred one."

Hope elbowed its way past the overwhelm. Though his words recalled the idea behind this Book Bulletin, Tatiana had lost sight of it in the pure logistics of the thing. But he was right. They weren't just packing up books, like the mail room did all year. They were delivering gifts meant to remind each person of the reason they celebrated, the ultimate Gift to humankind.

Perhaps, if she focused only on those logistics, it was a burden. Overwhelming. Impossible, even.

But if she focused on the purpose? The fact that she not only got to send her *own* book to so many households in

Iceland, but got to help them give innumerable other books too, books that would enrich them and touch their hearts? This wasn't a chore. It was an honor. It was the privilege of participating in something that could go on for years, something that could become a new tradition, if they did it well this year.

The thought of all the families that would be wrapping these books and exchanging them on Christmas Eve was enough to make the tears ebb. How many would do exactly what *she* always did when someone gave her a book for Christmas? Sit there beside their tree and start reading it before midnight Mass?

All they had to do was get the books to them in time. A challenge, yes. But one worth the effort it would take.

She turned to her uncle as Jon rolled a few carts over. "We'll have to divide and conquer, let those who know the mail systems take on the key roles but delegate anything else to the volunteers."

"Tatiana can focus on the order processing, like she's been doing," Bjarni said, "but then leave the fulfillment up to others. Her lists and spreadsheets have already been helpful in telling us what we'll need each day. We need her to focus solely on that, so we can hit the ground running each morning."

Jon began making neat stacks of envelopes to load onto the carts. "And we'll have to prioritize based on location, at this point. Those going farther need to be filled and sent out first. Local orders can go later and still arrive on time."

Valdi pointed a finger at Jon. "Smart thinking. We need to get a map in here and create zones. Check with the post office about normal delivery times within each one. That will tell us how long we have for the different regions' orders."

Mind whirling, Tatiana reached to shuffle envelopes into stacks as well. "So region first, then we'll break the orders down by contents and number of books, which will tell us how many of each size box or envelope we need, as well as the numbers of each title we'll have to fetch from the warehouse."

"Jon, you'll likely be making constant trips back and forth. If you need help to hurry the process along, let me know. We'll recruit someone." Valdi turned then to Bjarni. "While Tatiana is handling breaking down the orders themselves, I think your first step will be organizing the space down here to accommodate more people."

Calculations already spun through the man's eyes. "We'll need more tables. But I think I know where we can borrow some. I can have them here this evening."

"Perfect." Her uncle gave them all another confident smile. "Let's load up and go rally our rescuers, shall we?"

Tatiana gave her cheeks one more swipe and nodded.

FOUR

ANDERS FLEXED HIS FINGERS TO shake out the stiffness from too many hours with his pen in hand, looking up from the page to the clock on the wall and frowning. It was thirty minutes past when Tatiana had said she'd be back up from the warehouse and the shipping department, and it wasn't like her to be late.

His gaze drifted out the door into the outer office, where he'd set up a small desk for Elea—one he'd intended to give to his nephew for Christmas last year, but which Dalmar had nixed when he'd mentioned it to him. A veritable thundercloud had descended upon his brother's face too, as he'd said, *You'll not encourage the boy to spend any more time indoors at a desk. He'll be taking over the boat when he grows up. End of story.*

Though Anders had felt sympathy for ten-year-old Garri, who took after Anders more than his family would like, he hadn't dared cross Dalmar on the matter. There was no point. Had he given the desk, it just would have ended up tossed out anyway. So he'd kept it, thinking maybe his brother would eventually relent. Perhaps he could argue that it would be useful for Garri's schoolwork.

The battle had yet to be won, so Anders had hauled it in here yesterday and situated it across from Helga's desk. It was good to see some child putting it to use, anyway. Elea had been busy at it all day, working first on her homework from school and then on some drawing. She'd been so quiet that he'd forgotten she was there for much of the day, other than when Helga directed a question her way and he'd jolted to hear a young voice answer.

Now, he stretched, stood, and wandered to the doorway to give his neck and back a break from hunching over his own desk. He exchanged a smile with Helga and then sent it in Elea's direction and said, "Are you looking forward to Giljagaur coming tonight?"

She sent him a look that was part amusement, part disbelief. "You too? I thought only Aunt Tatta was so stuck on the idea of the Yule Lads still."

Tatiana had confessed to both him and Helga in whispers over the coffeepot this morning the conversation she and Elea had had the night before. So he could grin and point over his shoulder to the felt figures of the trolls he'd set up in his windowsill. They were one of the few decorations he brought to his office each year, solely because looking over and seeing them made up for the lack of sunlight coming through that window. "Giljagaur was always my favorite."

Elea stood from her desk and shifted to where she could see the line of silly trolls. "Because he's the tallest?"

"Because he's shy. So shy he wears disguises when he travels." Anders moved quickly to the windowsill to grab the felt doll and held it out for Elea as he leaned in the doorway again. "I have to say, I've considered it myself, now and then. Perhaps if I paste on a big white beard, my brothers won't recognize me and heckle me. What do you think?"

Elea giggled and ran her fingers through the wooly beard. "But he's responsible for feeding Jolakotturinn too—I wouldn't want to have to come close to that mean old Christmas Cat."

Anders made a show of considering. "I admit I was wary of the creature when I was a child, given my fear of becoming a snack. But now that I'm grown, he doesn't seem quite so intimidating. I have a cat of my own now, in fact. And she's only ever taken the tiniest nibbles of me."

At her desk, Helga grinned. A look of approval, one he seldom earned from the woman outside of business reasons.

The girl laughed again. "What's your cat's name?"

"Enja. She's a beautiful orange tabby. Who has never once threatened to eat naughty children if Giljagaur forgets to feed her." He winked and reached for one of the framed watercolors he kept on his desk, holding it out for inspection as well. He'd done this one of Enja when she was a mischievous kitten, sitting on the top of his highest bookshelf at home.

Elea set the doll down and reached for the picture, eyes wide as she crooned the universal approval of kittens. "She's so cute! Did you paint this?"

"I did." Another something his family had always called ridiculous—all those hours spent with sketching pencils and watercolor paints instead of tackle and nets. Thank the Lord for his grandmother, or he never would have had the art supplies to learn with. She'd been the sole member of his family to encourage his pursuit of the arts, and he missed her every day.

"I wish I was that good." Elea traced her gaze over each line of the painting.

Anders glanced to the desk with the many drawn-on papers on the top. "You have quite a lot of talent—every bit as much as I did at your age. If you spend time doing it, you will get better and better and soon be putting me to shame."

Her laugh was incredulous and flattered both. "I don't think so."

"Oh, I do. Come. Look." He turned back into his office and sat in his chair, opening the bottom drawer of his desk, where he'd stashed his eight-year-old illustrations for the same saga he was working on now—he'd brought them in as inspiration, thinking it would be fun to recreate them. He and Valdi were even debating including a few of his early sketches, side by side with his current artwork, in the back to show the children who'd read his book that they could chase their dreams.

Helga and Elea had both followed him in, shared curiosity on their faces that made him wonder if even his assistant was more interested in his personal work than he'd even dared to assume.

He cleared his throat. As always, it was easier to focus on the simple curiosity of a child than the complicated judgments of an adult. He directed his gaze to Elea. "I did this when I was older than you." He held out the drawing of Gunnar, most famous of all the Icelandic heroes of lore. "You see? You have a much better sense of anatomy and proportions than I did at your age."

She took the drawing, her grin going wider. "This is really yours?"

"Mm-hmm. Here's the version of the same scene I'm doing now." Another drawer pulled open, another sketch pulled out—this time the one he'd been working on during his lunch break yesterday. A bit more sophisticated than his childish version, to be sure, but clearly the same idea. The sketch was nearly done—he'd take it home with him tonight and start the painting.

She laughed in delight, which sparked a flame of warmth in his chest. *This* was why he ignored the prodding of his family. Defied generations of tradition. This was why he worked through every insecurity and doubt—to see that joy on a child's face and know he had put it there. To stir young hearts to embrace the bravery and courage of mythical heroes in their everyday lives. To help them realize that with faith and determination, they could do anything.

"Hey, Anders, Helga." One of the newest editors, Stig, leaned into the open doorway. "Boss wants us all in the common room for a minute." The young man sent a wink toward Elea, who'd turned to look at him. "He said you're welcome to come too, princess."

Helga immediately turned to follow Stig out. Elea set the drawing onto Anders's desk as he stood again from his chair, both of them following the others down the corridor, toward the bookcase-lined common area. Anders looked around the moment they entered, searching for Tatiana, but he didn't see her familiar golden curls anywhere.

Clearly Elea tried and failed in the same quest. No doubt failing to find either her aunt or grand-uncle was what inspired her to tuck her hand into his. He gave her fingers a reassuring squeeze and led her to a cozy corner of the room that Helga had staked out. All the seating was already taken by his colleagues.

They'd just turned back to face the room at large when Valdi and Tatiana both entered, each pulling a wheeled cart behind them. He wondered at first if this was some sort of Christmas gift exchange . . . but then he realized that all the objects in the carts were envelopes.

Familiar envelopes. All the same size and shape. All bearing the logo of the Book Bulletin on them.

His wasn't the only jaw that dropped. Were those all . . . orders? New ones?

Valdi turned to face his employees with a look of determination edged in panic. "Well, my friends. It seems we've done *too* good a job of advertising the Book Bulletin." He waved a hand at the overflowing mail carts. "These all arrived today. And we've promised Christmas delivery for any orders coming in through tomorrow. Who knows how many more we'll get then?"

Anders's gaze shifted from the cart to Tatiana. Her hair was a bit frazzled, and shadows had crept in under her eyes since he'd last seen her that morning.

"We'd thought that Tatiana in addition to the usual mail room staff would be able to handle the orders . . . but we clearly underestimated the success of the Bulletin. We've been flooded, as you can see."

"A book flood," Stig said, a grin pulling at his lips. "My kind of inundation."

Tatiana smiled too, despite the tired hand she'd lifted to shove away the hair that had broken free of its pins. "A *Christmas* book flood, even."

"A *jolabokaflod*," Valdi echoed, voice contemplative. A sparkle lit his eyes. "I like it. Next year, we'll call it that from the start. But to the point." He faced the crowd again. "We need volunteers downstairs. I know some of you are under tight deadlines already, and if that's the case, come speak to me about pushing things back by a week. But anyone who has the time, we could use your help."

Several of his colleagues' hands shot up immediately, murmurs of "I have the time" and similar exclamations sounding. Anders raised his hand too. He was ahead of schedule on the manuscript he was editing, and his next project—the second novel by Tandri Ebbisson—wasn't due until mid-January. There would be some spot checks and a proofread yet on other books, but nothing that would be incredibly time-consuming.

Tatiana's gaze flicked to him, then down and to the side, her lips curving up. He glanced over to see Elea had raised her hand as well, as had Helga—no surprise on his assistant. She could probably have the whole load of orders done before lunch and still get all his work done before she left for the day. With one hand tied behind her back. And the telephone glued to her shoulder.

"Wonderful," Valdi said, nodding at all the hands. "Thank you. Tomorrow we will be opening the office two hours early, and any who are willing can come in then or consider staying late. I of course understand that you have families and obligations, and I do not expect anyone to compromise that important time. But what hours you can spare, we will gladly take, and you will of course be compensated for them. And if you have family members who would be willing to help, the same goes for them. If they come, we'll happily pay them for their time." He picked an envelope up at random. "Our people are hungry for our books for Christmas. Let's make certain they get them in time."

A cheer went up and hands came together in applause. As they fell into a chatter of many conversations afterward, Anders stayed in his corner, especially when he saw Tatiana had aimed his way.

Well, her friend's and niece's way. But it was happily his direction too. She soon stood before them, and at this closer distance, he could see that she didn't just have shadows under her eyes—those eyes were red rimmed, as if she'd been crying.

Had she been crying? Why?

He'd never ask—but Elea apparently didn't have the same respect for privacy. "You look upset, Aunt Tatta."

Tatiana waved it away, but her sniffle sounded decidedly clogged, which spurred Helga to slip an arm around her shoulders and give her a squeeze. He tried not to be envious of the easy friendship the two women had, despite the decade gap in their ages. Tatiana said, "I had a moment of overwhelm when today's post arrived and I saw all I would be expected to do. But Uncle Valdi soon proved himself my hero and assured me I wouldn't be alone." Her gaze shifted to Anders. And did her cheeks flush, or was that just his imagination? "Thank you both for helping—again. I know you have more important things to do—"

"What could be more important than helping families give our books for Christmas?" He offered a smile, praying she would take it as comfort. Because she really wouldn't have to tackle that mountain of orders alone. And if he had to all but live at the office from now until Christmas, he was willing. Anything to keep the tears from her eyes.

And if doing so meant avoiding his family a bit . . . well, that was just an added bonus.

Guilt over the thought struck him as Tatiana turned back to her niece and knelt before her. She'd also confided at the coffeepot that Elea had been devastated at being sent away from her parents for Christmas, and here he was hoping for an excuse to dodge his mother and brothers and sister. He ought to be ashamed. Never mind that they didn't understand him. They were still his family. And after his father's death, he knew all too well that time was never guaranteed to them. He ought to focus more on loving them and less on being frustrated by them.

A subject he would have to devote to prayer, because no amount of effort thus far had managed to rid him of the frustration, despite the love that underscored it.

"Are you hungry?" Tatiana was asking Elea. "I'm sorry we'll be later leaving than usual. I don't know that we'll have time to make what I was planning for tonight, but we could stop at a restaurant on our way home. I'll plan something simple for tomorrow. And then on Thursdsay, Uncle Valdi said Aunt Beta would bring dinner to us here, and we can have a picnic. Won't that be fun?"

A picnic at the office wouldn't sound like fun to many children, but Elea smiled up at her aunt like the sweet thing she was. "Will we go and visit them at their house sometime too? I want to see the banana trees again."

"Banana trees?" He didn't mean to put himself into their conversation, but his surprise at that one couldn't be contained.

Tatiana laughed and straightened. "Yes, they've built a greenhouse around a geothermal vent, and it stays tropically warm in there. They've been growing bananas for several years—I'm surprised Uncle Valdi hasn't brought you any."

Anders's lips tugged up. "I suppose I've never rated so highly."

Still grinning, she shook her head. "That can't be it. You've probably mentioned not liking them at some point in his hearing."

How did *she* know that he didn't much care for bananas? He must have mentioned it in both of their hearings. Or perhaps Helga had shared it offhandedly at some point—she knew his preferences, given that she frequently brought baked goods to share. Though a glance at the older of the two blondes gave him no clues. "I may not like to eat them, but I'll have to finagle an invitation to the greenhouse someday. I'd love to see them growing."

"No finagling required." Valdi's voice came from behind him, and though it was cheerful and his boss's face was smiling, Anders still felt a flush creep up his neck at being caught inviting himself to the man's house. But Valdi knew him well. He chuckled and clapped a hand to his shoulder. "After we get these orders finished, I think a celebration will be in order anyway. I'll talk to Beta. I daresay she'll be amenable to inviting all the volunteers over for our annual Christmas party."

"A party!" Elea clapped and bounced a bit on her toes. For the first time since she'd come into the office that morning, the clouds fully cleared from her eyes. Tatiana surely noted it too, given the way her shoulders relaxed.

Valdi laughed. "That's right, *min kaera*. Perhaps you can help her plan it."

The little one's beaming smile erased any lingering embarrassment in Anders's chest, despite the fact that her enthusiasm was drawing the attention of all his colleagues within earshot. That was all right, though. It seemed that having a child around to try to please was enough to put smiles on every face, even with extra hours of work looming.

They'd all be exhausted by the time the last book was sent off in the post, he suspected. But it would be a well-earned exhaustion.

A few minutes later they were all bidding each other farewell. As Anders left the building, thoughts of Jolabokaflod, of Tatiana and Elea, and of his own family were still swirling through his mind like the snowflakes dancing over the pavement. Books, stories had brought light back to the little girl's eyes. That was why he loved them so.

Could he use them to bridge the gap between him and his family too? With the rationing, other gifts were hard to come by these last couple years, and though his family didn't put much stock in writing or illustrating or editing as a profession, they enjoyed reading as much as most other Icelanders.

Perhaps well-chosen books were the ticket to opening meaningful conversations with them. He certainly knew the Story Society catalogue backward and forward, and he could purchase any titles he wanted at a steep discount.

As he turned onto his street, a smile settled on his lips. He'd been wracking his brain trying to think up gifts for them that he could actually find, but after the lukewarm reception he'd received when he'd gifted them his *own* debut book, he'd never considered giving any of them books after that. He always asked them if they wanted a copy of his, but they always declined, frowns between their brows, as if he'd insulted them somehow.

But he needed to untangle himself from that equation. He needed to think not about how their opinions had hurt him, but about what they each loved. Adventure stories, perhaps Viking tales for Dalmar and Ulric and Ram. An impractical romance for his little sister, Ada, who always had such a thing stashed under her pillow to read when their stern mother wasn't looking. Their children's division had many new stories this year beyond his own that he could give to his nieces and nephews without drawing scowls of disapproval from his brothers. And for Mother . . . he'd have to give that one some thought. She read less than his father had, always claiming to be too busy. But now that Dalmar and his wife and their children had taken over the main house, she had fewer chores. Perhaps she'd enjoy one of the stories by a female author . . . although perhaps not. She didn't put much stock in these new ideas of fighting the patriarchy.

He pulled open the door to his building, jogged up the stairs, and let himself into his flat, considering all the while.

The answer came to him the moment he put his briefcase down and spotted the early copy of Tandri Ebbisson's debut novel, *By the Stars at Night*, sitting on his table. It would make the perfect gift for his mother—it had adventure, mystery, a dash of romance, and the sort of emphasis on family that she most loved. She was sure to enjoy it. And perhaps, after she'd read it, they could talk about it. Perhaps then he could admit to having worked with Tandri on it as his editor. That he even dared to count the reclusive author as a friend after their many letters—many of which had veered off topic and shared personal details, not just thoughts about the manuscript.

There was no guarantee it would work, of course. But it *could.* Perhaps it was time to obey the very advice he gave his authors. *Don't just tell the reader what happens. Show them.*

He'd been trying to tell his family for years why he'd chosen this life, why it meant so much to him. Time and again he'd broach the subject, and time and again they'd all go away frustrated.

This year, he would show them. Show them what he did every day. Show them why it mattered. Nearly every household in Iceland, after all, had responded to the Book Bulletin at this point—that must include his family. This year, perhaps they'd finally see why it was worthwhile.

FIVE

14 DECEMBER 1944

Tatiana laughed around the bite of leaf bread she'd taken, holding a hand to her mouth to keep the mirth from resulting in any crumbs from escaping. All around her, her colleagues were laughing too as Aunt Beta finished her story of her first disastrous Christmas as Valdi's wife, before she'd learned much by way of cookery. Tatiana had heard the story before, but that did nothing to make it less funny now.

Elea's laugh was brighter than all the adult versions, in that way that only children could manage. She giggled from deep inside, throwing her head back with the joy of it. She'd already finished the food she'd selected from the spread that Beta and several of the editors' wives had brought to feed the volunteers on this Thursday night, and though Tatiana had expected her niece to be either bored or impatient by this point in the day, Elea had surprised her.

She'd been working in the warehouse with Tatiana since after lunch the past two days, and she was nearly as fast as any of the other workers. In fact, after watching her for a few minutes earlier, Valdi had declared that she was working hard enough to earn some money for all her endeavors. Naturally, that had put a light in the girl's eyes and made her redouble her efforts. "I can buy presents to send home to Mamma and Pabbi," she'd declared in an excited whisper.

Tatiana had been all set to explain that the shops didn't have much to boast this year, given the rationing, but she ought to have known better. Elea had apparently been eyeing up some of the books on the company's shelves for her parents. She knew very well Valdi would have given their little helper any titles she wanted for her gift giving, but there was something special about earning them. Paying for them yourself. How could Tatiana argue with that?

There were two dozen of the Story Society's employees ranged around the warehouse floor, some on rickety folding chairs they'd scrounged from somewhere, others on the floor with their plates. Many of them had come in early that morning, just as she had, and those who couldn't were staying late. Some did both. Helga had been arriving early to help Tatiana on the processing and inventory management, attending to her usual duties with Elea at the small desk beside hers during the morning, then they'd both come down here after lunch. But she'd had to leave on time this evening to attend a program at her niece's school.

Tatiana and Elea had been there thirteen hours already, much like yesterday. It was a surprising amount of fun. Someone had brought in a record player and kept Christmas music piping through the warehouse all day, which lent a festive spirit.

Valdi and Beta's fifteen-year-old daughter, Camilla, picked her way through the picnicking employees and settled beside Tatiana and Elea with a grin. She'd come with her mother an hour ago to help with the food . . . and perhaps to try to convince her father to let her skip school the next day to help at the warehouse. Which Valdi had, of course, refused.

"Did Stufur come to see you last night, Elea?" Camilla flipped her braid of rich chestnut hair over her shoulder and focused her bright blue eyes on her little cousin.

Elea had given up rolling her eyes at all the people who asked her about the Yule Lads. She simply grinned and held out her wrist, showing off the macramé bracelet of red, green, and white that Tatiana had tucked into her shoe last night. "We had to set up a chair for him by the window so he could reach."

"Well of course you did." Camilla gave a serious nod. "Stufur means 'stubby,' after all. He's the shortest of the brothers. Did you leave *skyr* out for him?"

Elea shot Tatiana a grin. "Aunt Tatta made us stop at the grocer's and get some for him on our way home yesterday. We'd eaten the last of ours with breakfast."

Tatiana returned the smile with no apology. "Luckily, Stufur accepted our offering of store-bought yogurt. I wasn't so sure he would. When I was growing up on the farm, my mother always made her own *skyr* and claimed it was the only kind Stufur liked."

Elea's smile faded a bit. "Mamma likes to make it herself too. But she hasn't lately. She doesn't like the kind you can buy, though, so we just haven't had any."

These moments pounced without warning. Tatiana never knew what might lead to them—but she'd learned to either pivot or work with them. "I can't blame her. Our family's recipe is far better than what we can buy. But I never have time to make it myself either anymore." She turned her gaze to Camilla. "Does Aunt Beta make it fresh?"

Camilla had clearly also caught the sudden downturn of Elea's lips. She laughed. "Only for special occasions. She says that it's too much work when you don't have your own livestock to milk, like she did growing up. Living in the city requires change, she says. Personally, I'm so used to the store-bought variety that I think homemade *skyr* tastes funny."

Elea's eyes went wide in pure childish shock. "It's the *best*!"

"Says you." Camilla reached over to tickle Elea's side. Something or someone must have snagged the teenager's attention then, because she strained up a bit, her gaze tracking something from left to right. "I didn't realize Anders had stayed too."

"He's nice. He's been letting me do my schoolwork in his office in the morning, out with Helga, and he even showed me what he has of the Volsunga saga so far."

Camilla sent a questioning look to Tatiana. "How in the world is he making a child-friendly version of the Volsungs?"

Tatiana had to laugh at that, given that she'd wondered the same thing. The saga of that particular family was full of murder and infidelity and insatiable vengeance. But then again, so were the others that he'd successfully adapted for young readers. "The Vikings weren't exactly a peaceful people, were they?"

Camilla snorted her agreement.

"He let me read the story about Sigurth and the dragon, Fafnir. You should see his drawings! The dragon and his hoard of gold are so beautiful!" Elea turned back to her plate and picked up the cube of cheese she'd yet to eat.

Camilla's gaze was still off in the distance, presumably wherever Anders was. "I do find it curious that a man of such strong Christian faith chooses to tell stories about pagan Vikings that include their gods as characters."

Picking up her cup of water, Tatiana took a sip and smiled. "We tell stories of legends not because we believe they happened as they're told, but because they can teach us something true about ourselves and where we came from. The very fact that we now value things our ancestors didn't helps us understand *why* those values have changed. Plus," she added with a wink for Elea, "they're good fun. Aren't they?"

"Like the Yule Lads." Elea grinned. "Pottasleikir is coming tomorrow morning. I told Aunt Tatta she had better leave her dishes unwashed so he can lick the pots clean. Anders's little felt troll set has one holding a pot for Pottasleikir."

Their cousin's brows went up. "Anders has little felt Yule Lads?"

"In his office," Elea confirmed with a nod.

"How . . . whimsical." Camilla said it as though it were the highest compliment one could pay to a man.

And she had a point. The fact that he brought in the trolls for Christmas, that he had painted a picture of his kitten, that he spent time thinking up ways to make the old legends accessible to today's children were some of the things she loved about him.

Liked. Things she *liked* about him. A few dozen letters over the course of a year could not make one fall in love with someone, especially when that someone thought he was corresponding with a man.

"He's been so nice." Elea's face was as bright as the summer sun. She leaned close to their cousin and stage-whispered, "I think it's for Aunt Tatta. I think he *likes* her."

Tatiana choked on the sip of water she'd just taken, coughing into her hand and regretting it as countless eyes turned her way.

"Are you all right, Tatta?" Camilla patted her on the back, concern in her voice.

Elea, the little imp, just grinned. "I think she likes him too."

"Hush," Tatiana barely managed to squeak out around another ridiculous cough. She tried to wave away the attention with a hand and a grin, assuring her colleagues that she was fine—if foolish. A few more coughs and throat clearings and she had it mostly under control. Elea and Camilla were both staring at her, expectation etched into their expressions. Clearly they had no intention of letting her off the hook just because of a little thing like breathing in fluid. "Of *course* I like him," she said quietly. "He's an admirable man, one I respect immensely. And he is merely kind and thoughtful. It isn't that he thinks of me in any special way."

Camilla drew her bottom lip between her teeth, but it did little to hold back her smile.

Elea didn't bother trying. "He watches you all the time. And always finds an excuse to be wherever you are."

"Nonsense. We work together, that's all. And he's keeping tabs on me right now only because of *you*, Elea." That was all—it must be. They'd been working together for five years, after all, and he'd never so much as asked her to dinner. And why would he? He was one of the most brilliant literary minds of their day, and for all he knew, she was nothing but a backwater farm girl on whom her uncle had taken pity, one suited to nothing but sorting mail and answering the telephone.

"You *would* make a handsome couple," Camilla murmured, eyes alight with mischief.

Tatiana did her best to return her face to neutral. The last thing she needed was her cousin and niece realizing that they were naming the very thing she'd begun to dream of. It would make it all the harder to face reality if someone knew that dream. Just like the dream of writing. "We are not a—"

"Hey, Anders!" Elea jumped to her feet, and Tatiana couldn't be sure if it was genuine excitement or a kindhearted way to interrupt her as Anders apparently picked his way through the crowd toward them.

Turning half around, Tatiana saw the smile he gave her niece, and her ridiculous heart melted all the more for him. Why did he have to be so absolutely perfect?

He nodded to both Tatiana and Camilla but quickly returned his attention to Elea as he reached them. "Guess what I have just learned?"

Elea was always happy to play along. "What?"

"There is a party for children on Saturday, hosted by the Americans at Camp Kwitcherbelliakin."

When the Americans first set up camp, Tatiana hadn't known enough English to understand the strange name. But Stig was fluent and had explained the play on words to her, that it sounded like "Quit your bellyaching" . . . a decidedly American idiom about complaining, it seemed. Now she couldn't hear the name without chuckling. Elea clearly didn't get the joke, but she tilted her head at the prospect of a party. "What kind of party?"

"Well if it's like years past, there will be someone dressed up as St. Nicholas. They will sing Christmas songs and have games, and there will be cake and chocolate."

Elea had been too young to remember life before the war began, but she certainly knew that chocolate, rare as it now was, was one of her favorite things. She spun to Tatiana. "Can we go, Aunt Tatta? Can we?"

She'd been planning on spending Saturday readying the flat for Christmas and using her saved-up rations to do some

Christmas baking. And she'd never actually gone to the American base—fraternizing with the foreign men had been highly discouraged, even though the soldiers seemed rather desperate to have local girls come to their dances. The very thought of taking Elea there alone was daunting, to say the least. But how could she turn her niece down?

Anders sent her a warm smile. "I thought I could take the two of you, if you're not too busy. I was talking to my mother on the phone just now and promised to take my niece, and I believe she and Elea are about the same age. I thought they'd like to meet each other. None of my nephews want to go, and Heidi is eager for a companion."

Camilla leaned close enough to whisper into Tatiana's ear, "You had *better* snap him up, Tatta. He couldn't be more perfect!"

As if it were that easy.

Elea, of course, bounced in delight. "I'd love to! Can we, Aunt Tatta?"

In all likelihood, she asked because she really wanted to go. But Tatiana wasn't entirely willing to dismiss the possibility that her mischievous little niece was trying to play miniature matchmaker.

And was the gaze Anders sent her way warmer than usual, or was that just her imagination, fed by Elea's claims of preference on his part?

Well, her plans for the day had been solely for Elea's benefit anyway. They could do the baking another time. "Of course. We'd be delighted to join you."

"Wonderful. The party begins at two o'clock. Heidi and I will drop by your flat and fetch you at one thirty." He fell into awkwardness for a moment, nodding and half turning away, then back, then finally shaking his head and leaving with a wave . . . and a flush creeping up his neck.

She couldn't help but smile at his retreating form. If there were a dearer man in Iceland, she'd never met him.

And given the way Elea and Camilla were giggling and nudging each other as they watched her, her admiration was clear on her face. She felt her own cheeks heat in response and rolled her eyes. "Don't say it," she ordered in as gruff a voice as she could manage around her laugh. She pushed to her feet and nodded to the stack of orders they still had to get through today, if they were going to get them all out in time for Christmas delivery. "Another half hour or so of work, I think."

The three of them headed for the worktable and got to it.

SIX

14 DECEMBER 1944

It was more than a little pathetic that he'd gotten so little sleep last night because he was agonizing over a children's Christmas party still more than twenty-four hours away. But knowing that hadn't kept the thoughts from endlessly parading through Anders's mind as he'd lain in bed. Had it just been Elea joining him and Heidi, it would have been fine. But Tatiana was coming too.

It would be the first time they'd done anything together outside of work. For that matter, it would be the first time in years he'd done *anything* with a woman who wasn't a relative outside of work. Just a children's party, true. Not a date, per se.

He'd tried telling that to his overactive imagination time and again, but still it kept presenting him with innumerable scenarios for ways he could mess it all up and make Tatiana storm off in disgust.

From her little desk, Elea gusted out a sigh that was frustrated enough to capture his attention—attention that *should* have been on the manuscript before him, not on what stupid thing he'd likely say tomorrow to make Tatiana wish she'd stayed at home. He stood and moved to his door. Helga had been rising too but paused when she spotted him and gave him an encouraging nod. "Everything all right, Elea?"

She smacked her pencil on the desk. "It's all wrong. What am I doing wrong?" She held up the paper she'd been drawing on—she'd already finished all the schoolwork her teacher had sent with her, but they'd still decided she'd spend the morning with him and Helga rather than in the warehouse, so she didn't exhaust herself.

Anders moved closer and studied the drawing. He could tell at a glance that the figures represented Elea and . . . a woman. The little girl on the page had two braids just like Elea and was wearing a dress like the one she currently had on. But he couldn't be sure if the woman was meant to be her mother or her aunt. At least not at first. But further study showed him the skirt suit he highly doubted her mother wore on the farm.

"You and your aunt?"

She nodded but huffed again. "The hands are all wrong. And I can't get the typewriter right either."

Ah . . . was that what the awkwardly shaped box in the background was? He smiled. "Hands are notoriously tricky.

I always put people in mittens in my drawings when I was your age to avoid the problem."

She giggled at that. "That makes sense for winter. But what about summer pictures?"

"They always had their hands behind their back." He hid his in demonstration. "Problem solved."

This time her laugh was full and bright. "You draw hands now though. And they always look perfect."

"Because eventually I decided I had better master them, so I drew them every day. Just hands—hands in every position I could think of. I'd sit like this." He put his left hand into a pose and picked up a pencil with his right, mimicking drawing the left. "Of course, that meant I got good at left hands and still had trouble for a while with rights. My mother was forever frustrated by the bodiless hands strewn all over our house—though she said it was better than my eye phase." He grinned at the memory. "Everywhere she turned around, there was a paper with an eye staring at her. Angry eyes, dreamy eyes, surprised eyes . . ."

Helga laughed. "Your poor mother! All those dismembered body parts."

Elea grinned. "You must have practiced a lot."

"Much to my parents' dismay." He motioned for her to lower the drawing to the desk again and knelt beside her. "As for the typewriter—you're drawing what your mind says it should look like rather than what your eyes actually see. If viewing a typewriter from this angle, you don't actually see the roundness of the keys, do you? Take a look." He motioned toward the machine on his own desk.

She got up and moved into his office, going behind his desk, brows furrowing as she studied it. "The keys just look . . . flat. Maybe a little bit of an oval on some of them."

"Mm-hmm. This is what we call 'perspective' in art. And you needn't feel bad for not realizing it—it wasn't until the Renaissance that artists began incorporating perspective into their work. Realism didn't always matter, you see. And there are plenty of artistic movements that don't care about realism even today."

"I want it to look real though." She pursed her lips, eyes still on the typewriter. "Can I look at this while I'm drawing it?"

"Certainly. I'll set it on Helga's desk for you so you can see it." He rose from his kneel and did just that. It wasn't as though he needed the typewriter this morning anyway, and while Helga had one of her own, she *was* using it.

Though as he got it into its new position, he paused, his own brows drawing together. Tatiana had a typewriter in her office, it was true, which she used for the correspondence she did for Valdi, much as Helga did for Anders. But from the details Elea had already lightly sketched into place, the room she and Tatiana were standing in was *not* her aunt's office at the Story Society. The desk was completely different, and there was a sofa visible too, and a window. "Is this your aunt's flat?"

"Mm-hmm." Elea scurried back to her seat.

"She has a typewriter at home?" Not entirely odd, he

supposed . . . but not entirely common, either. No one in *his* family had one, certainly not that they kept out on display.

Elea nodded and picked up her pencil again. "She's on it all the time—always typing when I get up, and once I've gone to bed too. Even now, when we have to leave so early and get home so late."

Anders's brows lifted. That didn't sound like correspondence, though he supposed it could have been. Perhaps she had a lot of friends from their village to write letters to. "What is she writing?"

Elea shrugged. "A story, but she wouldn't tell me more than that."

He glanced to Helga, but she looked just as surprised by the information as he felt.

His pulse kicked up—he couldn't help it. The mention of story writing always did that to him, whether it was one he was working on, one he was editing, or one he was simply hearing about. And the thought of Tatiana writing a story . . . excitement bubbled. It could give them something to talk about. Something else they had in common. Perhaps he could even help her somehow—if ever she admitted her writing to him, he could offer. Perhaps they could have a little critique partnership. Get together for coffee and reading and talk about plots and characters and . . . and he'd probably make some suggestion that she would hate and then she'd resent him and think him idiotic and heavy-handed, and then instead of seeing her *more*, she'd avoid him even at the office and . . .

There he went again. Why was his imagination always so quick to think up worst-case scenarios?

Elea paused suddenly, turning her face his way. "Have *you* ever drawn Aunt Tatta?"

And now heat climbed his neck and stained his cheeks. He turned back to his door in the hopes that the little girl wouldn't notice. "No, I haven't." It was true. He hadn't dared, not with how often his family dropped by without warning. If they saw a drawing of a beautiful modern woman, they'd tease him endlessly. And he certainly couldn't work on such a thing *here*.

But he'd mentally composed any number of drawings. Some portraits, others candid. Occasionally he'd imagined her as the beautiful Brynhild, sporting gleaming chain mail and her warrior's sword, or the determined Signy, or the young Sigrun. Though inevitably he decided not to cast her in any of those tragic roles—it seemed all the heroes and heroines of the old sagas met violent ends, something he usually neglected to include in his children's versions. But still, *he* knew how the real tales went, and he had no desire to imagine anyone he admired taking on those roles.

Elea turned on her chair to face him, eyes alight. "Would you draw one of me and Aunt Tatta too? I was going to give her mine for Christmas—you could too. It would be fun! A way to remember my visit."

He ought to decline—after all, he hadn't time for random drawing. He had editing to do in the morning, books to help pack up in the afternoon and evening, and his own next manuscript to write and illustrate over the weekends.

Yet the mere suggestion was enough to make a scene jump into his mind, and his lips twitched into a smile as he returned to his desk chair. He imagined Tatiana in that red suit she wore so often this time of year, in profile, holding a stack of books that towered far too high. Beside her would be Elea, standing on a stack of books rather than carrying them, giving her enough height to peek over her aunt's shoulder at the title on the top of the stack. The snowy city behind them, with the aurora dancing in the background, a few snowflakes drifting down.

Bother. Now he had no choice but to pull out a piece of watercolor paper from the stack he always kept in a drawer—one never knew when inspiration would strike over a lunch or coffee break—and grab his favorite sketching pencil. He imagined this one almost in the style of the American Norman Rockwell, though not with the earthy color scheme Rockwell often chose. No, he imagined deep blues and bold reds and then that dance of pastels in the sky.

He would grant himself fifteen minutes—the amount of time he could have taken for a coffee break, since it was time for one anyway. Not enough time to really get the details down, and certainly not time enough for painting. But enough to get the rough image onto paper, anyway. Light strokes that would be covered up with paint. Straight lines for the books, soft curves for the females. A dreamy expression on Tatiana's face as she looked up at the night sky, all those books in her arms. An inquisitive one for Elea, so eager to learn and understand. Once he added color, he'd give Tatiana red lips to match her skirt and jacket. Elea he'd put in the green dress she'd worn her first day here, with the crisp white blouse beneath it. Together they would look like Christmas.

He kept glancing at his watch as he worked, so that when his self-imposed time had run out, he put his pencil down again. His gaze moved critically over the drawing. It was hasty, yes, and he could see several things he'd tweak before he put color to it. But it was close enough to his vision to make him grin. He held it up for Elea to see through the doorway. "What do you think?"

She'd given up on her own work and had moved to stand in front of his desk at some point. He hadn't even noticed, but she must have been watching him for a while. Her grin was quick and bright. "That's . . . that's just *perfect*. It's *us*!"

"We'll call it *Jolabokoflod*."

Elea clapped. "Uncle Valdi should use it for an advertisement next year!"

He laughed, because Valdi had never once asked him to develop any art for advertising . . . but it wasn't a bad idea, really. With the success of the Book Bulletin, it was quite possible that they'd want artwork for it in the future. He didn't want to presume anything, of course. But knowing Elea as he'd begun to do, she'd suggest it to her uncle without any help from Anders.

Which was perfect, really. She'd plant the idea, and if Valdi liked it, he'd bring it up to Anders. If not, it could be waved off as a little girl's fancy, no hard feelings on either side.

For now, he set the paper aside. "All right, enough of that. I had better get back to work so that I can help in the warehouse again after lunch."

Elea nodded. "Me too. Once I get the typewriter fixed, I still need to color it all in." She motioned to the box of colored crayons she'd brought with her today.

He granted her a serious nod. "Indeed. And after you've finished, I can help you frame it, if you like. I have plenty of them at home." Once upon a time he too had given drawings to family members, so had begun buying up frames whenever he saw them for a bargain. But after realizing they never displayed any of them, he'd given up. Which meant he still had quite a stack of frames and only so much space on his own walls.

"Really?" Elea's eyes twinkled. "And you'll frame that one too? Aunt Tatta's going to *love* it!"

He nodded, even as his stomach churned at the thought. He'd never given Tatiana a gift. They exchanged names at the office, but he'd never drawn hers—and even if he had, that would have been different. This . . . this was a voluntary gift. A personal gift. It meant feelings were on the line. It meant . . . *something*. Giving a gift to a beautiful young woman—other than family—was momentous, wasn't it? He'd never done it before. He'd taken ladies out on a few dates over the years, of course, but none had ever turned into relationships that lasted through Christmas.

Yet another reason his brothers taunted him and his mother was perpetually disappointed. Anders the Red-Faced

Bookworm was a lost cause in their minds. He'd never actually convince a woman to marry him, despite the fact that he thought he'd make a decent husband and father. *Women don't want a man who has his nose always stuck in a book*, Ulric had pointed out just a few months ago. *Don't you learn anything from those sagas you read nonstop? They want strong men, capable of providing for them with the work of their hands. They want men willing to fight for them, if it comes down to it.*

Much as he wanted to think modern women were a bit more enlightened than all that and *didn't* rate potential husbands solely on their height or musculature or propensity to get into fistfights, it was hard to argue with the elder brothers who outdid him physically in every way. Who'd never shied away from a brawl, and who had all been married by the age of twenty-five.

Although let it be noted, Valdi was a bookworm too, and he had a wife and family who seemed happy with him. So perhaps there was hope for Anders yet.

He slipped his sketch into his briefcase, and not a moment too soon. The familiar sound of Tatiana's heels clicking on the tile floor sounded, Helga called out a greeting that was no doubt a warning, prompting Elea to cover up her drawing with another she'd begun of the Yule Lads. A moment later, Tatiana's beautiful blonde head peeped into the outer office, a smile on her lips. "How's it going in here?"

Helga didn't miss a beat. "Wonderfully. We should be ready to join you in the warehouse after lunch. How are things with the shipping department?"

She sighed, but it didn't erase the happy gleam in her eyes. "We'll be cutting it close, but I think we're on track. All the orders that have farther to go should be in the post today and Monday. That only leaves the local deliveries within Reykjavik and the surrounding towns to finish up next week."

"Ten days until Christmas." Elea flashed a smile, though Anders didn't miss the sorrow that underscored it, and he suspected Tatiana didn't either. The little girl drew her lip between her teeth. "Mamma's doctor is coming to visit today. Do you think he's been there yet? I hope . . . I hope the baby's okay."

Tatiana moved fully into the outer office so she could smooth a hand over her niece's hair. "We'll call her when we get home this evening. And whenever you start to worry, let it remind you to pray." She offered a small smile. "That's what I've been doing."

A good reminder for Anders too. He'd been praying for Ari every time he saw the worry overtake Elea—*that* was easy to remember. What proved harder was remembering to offer his own faults to the Lord. When his thoughts spiraled like they did every time he thought of Tatiana, into all the ways he could alienate her, he never seemed to recall that he should pray about it instead.

Maybe that was why he'd gone five years without braving more than idle chitchat over the coffeepot. Why he'd never dared ask her to dinner or a movie.

If his brothers were to be believed, he ought instead to take a page from the Volsungs and just stride up to her and say, *You're the most beautiful and wise woman in the world, and I will spend my life with no one but you. You must marry me, because I want no other.*

Right. Because *that* approach was sure to work for the average man.

Clearly oblivious to his thoughts, she turned to him with an easy smile. "I brought soup and bread for lunch. Helga's joining us, and you're welcome too, Anders. I have it heating in the break room."

Were it not for the little one looking at him with such friendly acceptance, he probably would have hemmed and hawed and made an excuse to decline, lest he make a fool of himself. Within two seconds, he'd have convinced himself that she only issued the invitation out of a sense of duty, a way of thanking him for helping with her niece. That it wasn't a *genuine* invitation, and that she didn't really *want* him to accept. But given Elea's hopeful expression, he shoved aside the self-doubts and found the courage to smile. "I . . . thank you. I'd be delighted."

Tatiana beamed a smile at him. One bright enough that he almost wondered . . . almost thought . . . almost dared to dream that she was as happy he'd said yes as he was.

SEVEN

16 DECEMBER 1944

Tatiana craned her head to watch the PBY *Catalina* fly overhead, closer than she ever got to see them in the city. She walked backward for a few steps so that she could keep it in view as it aimed toward the runway at the American base, a few of the day's last rays of sunlight glinting off its wings. Airplanes never ceased to amaze her. How they could strap engines to giant tin cans and get them airborne was completely beyond her.

"They say someday airplanes will be so common that everyone will be able to fly on them, if they want," Anders said from beside her.

A thought ridiculous enough to make her laugh. Oh, she knew that plenty of people flew these days, and Reykjavik had boasted an airport since 1919—but it wasn't exactly accessible to common people. She couldn't imagine spending the money on such a thing. Nor could she imagine actually going up in the air in one of those tin cans.

She took another backward step—but shouldn't have. Her booted foot found a pothole and a squeal escaped her lips as she lost her balance. Her arms wheeled out, and she would have fallen gracelessly to the ground had Anders not steadied her with an arm around her back. She looked over and up at his face, closer than she'd ever been to him before, and smiled into the warm light in his eyes. "My hero," she said around another laugh.

He should grin more often. When he did, it made his eyes shrink to glistening crescents that invited her to memorize the shade of blue his irises were. He helped her regain her feet and then, after a moment of clear indecision, offered his elbow. "Perhaps to . . . steady you?"

She'd be plenty steady once she faced forward again, but she wasn't about to turn down the offer. Pivoting with him back toward the city and the two little girls skipping happily a few feet ahead of them, she tucked her mittened hand into the crook of his elbow. "Thank you."

Though his scarf covered much of his neck, she thought she glimpsed just a bit of red rising above it into his face. He cleared his throat and nodded toward their nieces. "Glad they hit it off so quickly."

She smiled, having thought the same. "Elea is always quick to make friends. She takes after her father in that. Ari and I were both always a bit more introverted."

"Someone who loves books and art but is still an extrovert. She's a veritable unicorn."

Another laugh bubbled up. She'd never heard a unique person being described as a mythical creature before, but it fit. "I can't thank you enough for all your help with her this week. As sad as she was when she arrived, I thought for sure this would be a visit full of tears and anger—but instead, she's been all but bursting with stories every day when we get home."

It reminded her of her own childhood, how she and Ari would race home from school to tell their parents all the day's stories. She'd spend the entire journey trying to figure out how to weave all the little minutiae of her day into a tale with a beginning, a middle, and an end, one that exaggerated the adventures with friends or the villainy of her rivals. And their parents would listen with rapt attention, with laughter or gasps, and then compose their own stories to share.

She'd missed that. In general, living alone hadn't proven to be as lonely as she feared it would be, but having Elea with her for more than just a weekend . . . it made her remember how much she loved having a family around her. People to share her day with. People to listen to each other's stories. It made her yearn for children of her own to engrain with the love of storytelling that all Icelanders seemed to be born with, to a greater or lesser degree.

"You don't need to thank me," Anders said. *Of course.* "Helga is the true hero, making her so comfortable. But for my part, it has been a joy, and I have no doubt next week will be as well. Children always have such a fresh way of looking at things, don't they?"

She nodded her agreement, smiling when Heidi, just a few months older than Elea, turned back for a second to make sure they were still there and flashed a grin at her uncle that declared without words that he was her favorite.

And no wonder. Tatiana had already learned today that, since Anders's three brothers were out fishing every day but Sundays, he was often the one to step in on Saturdays and take the children on outings. From the sound of it, scarcely a weekend went by when he wasn't fulfilling the role of doting uncle with at least one niece or nephew, and often three or four at a time. He had a total of eight, she'd learned—five boys and three girls, though two of those girls were under the age of three, so not yet good companions for Heidi. Hence why she'd been so thrilled when he'd said Elea would be joining them.

For a moment, she let herself imagine that they weren't just colleagues, she and Anders. That they were a real couple walking along the road from the American base back to the city, that Heidi and Elea were truly cousins. Or, better still, their own daughters, laughing and chattering away like she and Ari had always done.

A silly dream. But one so potent she knew she'd better dislodge it from her mind pronto. She turned her face up toward his. "Do you have plans with your family for Christmas?"

"Mm." His agreement didn't sound exactly exuberant. "There will be dinner on Christmas Eve at my mother's, as always. We'll exchange our gifts, then go to the midnight service at church."

She lifted her brows. "You don't sound excited."

He sighed, keeping his gaze focused on the girls. "It's just . . . sometimes I feel more alone with my family than I do when I'm actually alone." He darted his eyes toward her, then forward again. "That probably sounds ridiculous. I'm blessed to have them. I know that. But . . ."

"But when you're different from them, you can feel so very out of place in their company." She nodded. "I've thought the same on occasion. Don't get me wrong—I love my family, and we've always gotten along well. But they're all perfectly content with life in our little village, where they run our farm or spend their days fishing. Where my mother and sister busy themselves all day long with housekeeping tasks and find joy in it."

Well—Ari's joy had been hard to come by in the last few years, but it wasn't because she didn't find the life of a farmer's daughter and fisherman's wife fulfilling. It was just the grief of losing so many babies to miscarriage.

Tatiana sighed. "I knew that wasn't the life for me. I tried so hard to imagine it, tried to fall in love with someone from the village, tried to pretend that was all I wanted in life—but it just *wasn't*." She shrugged, daring a quick peek up at Anders and finding his gaze steady on her, despite the fact that they kept walking. "So I wrote to Uncle Valdi and all but begged him to give me a job. An opportunity to move to the city, to work with books." To learn how to write them, though she wasn't about to confess that. "Not that I don't want a family someday, of course." Too pointed? She hoped not.

His smile said he understood perfectly. "We are more alike than I thought. My family all lives in Reykjavik, of course, but they have been fishermen for generations, both sides. I'm the oddball too." He sent her another smile, then looked forward again, clearing his throat. "And I am . . . quite glad your uncle gave you a job. You . . . you bring sunshine into the office."

She knew very well his cheeks would be reddening if she looked over at him, and since she felt her own flush, she instead kept her face forward. But she leaned a little closer, so that their arms brushed. Anders was always kind, but that was by far the most personally complimentary thing he'd ever said to her, and she knew it had cost him to say it.

For the first time, she wondered if Elea was right. Maybe he *did* like her. Maybe the fact that he'd never said anything was more because he was bashful than because he saw her as nothing but her uncle's assistant.

Her pulse thundered in her ears. She should encourage him. Make it clear that she'd welcome it if he ever decided to ask her on an outing without the excuse of their nieces.

Of course, if they were to date, then she'd have to confess that they were already more than office colleagues—that he was, in fact, her editor. That the rapport they'd developed via correspondence was *theirs*.

It made anxiety knot her stomach, and she realized as the first buildings of town rose up around them that she'd waited too long to respond. Which triggered a whole new anxiety—she didn't want him to think his opinion wasn't treasured, but they had only minutes left of their walk.

She lifted her free hand and rested it against his forearm, sending him a warm smile. "This has been so nice. I'm glad you asked us to come."

His face turned her way, a smile upon his lips—but then it froze, and his posture shifted as his gaze fastened on something beyond her. She turned too and saw that they'd drawn even with the building he'd pointed out as his on their way out of town, and that two women were standing outside the door, the older of them even now lifting her hand in greeting.

His mother, she could see that at a glance. And the younger woman beside her looked exactly like her, minus thirty years, which meant it must be his little sister, Ada. And given the confusion on their faces, clearly neither of them had a clue who she or Elea were.

"Anders," his mother called out in greeting as he adjusted course. "Heidi."

The girls spun toward the building too, Heidi shouting, "Ommu!" and rushing to wrap her arms around the woman.

Tatiana considered drawing her arm from Anders's . . . but if he'd wanted her to, he would have lowered his, releasing her. The fact that he held his arm steady made her think he didn't mind his mother seeing them walking like this, together. And it wasn't just curiosity in the woman's gaze, unless Tatiana was mistaken. It was intrigue. Excitement, even.

"Who are your friends?" his mother asked in a tone that implied, *And why didn't I know you were taking a woman and another little girl with you today? Have you been hiding things from me?*

Tatiana smiled. Mothers were the same, it seemed, wherever they were.

Anders cleared his throat. "Mother, this is Tatiana, Valdi's niece. She works as the publisher's assistant at the Story Society. And this is her niece, Elea. I thought Heidi would enjoy making a new friend so invited them to join us. Tatiana, Elea, allow me to introduce my mother, Gilla, and my sister, Ada."

They exchanged hellos, Gilla's gaze moving from her son to Tatiana and back again, clearly trying to discern what might be between them. But she said only, "It looked as though you'd intended to walk on by—were you seeing Tatiana and Elea home?"

"Of course. Then I was going to take Heidi home to Ram's house."

His mother beamed. "I was just saying I could use a walk. We'll join you."

There was no refusing such an invitation, but Tatiana didn't mind the new additions, even when it somehow resulted in her hand losing its place wrapped around Anders's arm when the little girls darted between them in a game of chase. In the ensuing laughter, Ada ended up beside her brother and Tatiana beside Gilla, since the sidewalk wasn't large enough to walk more than two abreast.

"How long have you been working at the Story Society?" Gilla asked with a smile that said she'd maneuvered them exactly to her liking.

Tatiana had no trouble keeping her own smile fresh. If it were *her* parents who had found them instead of his, she knew very well Pabbi or Mother would be angling for a conversation with him too. "Five years now. I was so excited to be hired—and your son is a large part of that."

She knew very well he could hear her, and the fact that he almost tripped over his own feet told her he was more than a little surprised by her words. Her smile turned into a grin. "I've long admired his writing and illustrating, and my uncle had told me that he'd been the lead editor on several of my favorite books. I couldn't believe I'd actually get to *meet* him! You must be so proud. Uncle Valdi is forever saying how Anders is one of the most brilliant literary minds of our day, and I thoroughly agree."

Gilla sent an indulgent smile toward her son's back. "Always smart as a whip, Anders was. So much cleverer than the rest of us. I knew he'd do great things."

Anders darted an incredulous look over his shoulder.

Tatiana leaned closer to Gilla and pitched her voice low. "And handsome too." She didn't really care, just now, if he heard her.

Which was good, because his mother's laugh was full volume, as was her, "Oh, *all* my sons are handsome. They take after their father." A wistful look overtook her face, and she let out a long breath. "I still miss him. Anders made a painting of the two of us, you know—gave it to us for Christmas just a month before my Johann died. We'd been debating where to hang it, but after that . . . I had Dalmar hang it in my bedroom for me, so it would be the first thing I see every morning when I wake up, and the last thing before I turn out the lights. He *captured* him. Us." Her smile went a bit mischievous as she looked back to Tatiana. "You'll have to come and visit sometime. I'll show it to you."

"I'd love to see it," she said, trying to decipher why in the world Anders was goggling over his shoulder at them *now*, as if in total confusion. Was he perhaps surprised that his mother would issue the invitation on so short an acquaintance? He surely knew it was the fact that they'd been walking arm in arm that had sparked Gilla's interest in Tatiana. "He has a few of his drawings at the office, and I can never get enough of seeing them."

"He did some for his brothers too, that same year, and their wives all took the cue from me and hung them up in their bedrooms. I'd hoped he'd make a tradition of giving us artwork each year, but . . ." She shrugged. "He's been kept so busy, now that his sagas are being published. His brothers and I visit him a few times a week just to make sure he's not working too hard to keep himself fed."

Ada was clearly listening in as well. She sent a smile over her shoulder at them and then bumped her shoulder into Anders's arm. "Well, I'm going to commission a wedding portrait from him. You'll paint me and Obi, won't you, Anders? It can be the first piece of art we have in our new home."

"I . . ." He frowned at his sister. "Of course I will. If you want me to."

She rolled her eyes as only a sister could. "Of *course* I want you to. Mother said I shouldn't ask, but why not? If a little sister can't pester her talented big brother, then what's the point?"

Tatiana laughed. Anders did not. He shook his head slowly, as if trying to make sense of something.

"He gets pestered enough by his brothers. Boys," Gilla said with a smile and a shake of her own head that didn't look nearly so confused as her son's. "His brothers give him such a hard time—of course, they give each *other* a hard time too. It's the way they show their affection, but I've never understood it."

"I only have the one sister," Tatiana said. "But I have scads of male cousins and have observed this about them. I've never understood it either. Why can't they just say nice things to each other once in a while?"

Gilla laughed. "It's as if they think the sky will fall."

The little ones, who had been leading the way, darted around Anders and Ada, Heidi grabbing at her grandmother's hand. "Ommu, can Elea and her aunt come to your house for Christmas Eve? Can they? Please?"

Now Tatiana's cheeks warmed again. She had been debating what to do on Christmas Eve—to have a quiet evening with just her and Elea or to go to Valdi and Beta's, as she'd originally planned. But nowhere in the debate had there been any intention of inviting themselves somewhere else entirely.

Gilla didn't bat an eye, just grinned at her granddaughter. "Of course they're welcome, if they could squeeze us in around the other plans they probably already have."

Heidi didn't seem to hear the part about other plans. She just clapped and darted forward again, calling out, "You can come!"

Tatiana let out a breath of laughter.

Gilla sent her a wink. "No obligation, of course. But you truly are welcome. Heidi is always complaining about the lack of girl cousins near her age for her to play with. Which neighborhood is your niece from? Perhaps we can get them together more often."

"Oh, she's only visiting Reykjavik," Tatiana said. "My family lives in Hellnar, about three hours away."

Gilla's eyes lit. "A fishing village!"

"Once the biggest," she agreed with a nod. "Elea's father is a fisherman, though he and my sister are also running my family farm. My parents have retired to a little cottage in the village proper where they can help care for my grandmothers more easily." She knew very well that it was only because Mother and Pabbi had their hands full with their two mothers, neither of whom was in good health, that Ari had asked Tatiana to help with Elea instead of their parents. Gunnar's parents both worked punishing hours at the fishery.

Gilla gave her a big smile and looped their arms together. "I assumed you were from the city, one of the academic types Anders runs with."

Her own smile felt a bit self-deprecating on her lips. "I only just moved here five years ago. Though my uncle has called Reykjavik home for about twenty-five years now. Since my father was more interested in keeping the farm than he was, Valdi went to university and then stayed here afterward. It worked out well for everyone."

"A girl who understands all the publishing things but has roots in Hellnar." Gilla patted her arm. "Anders, I like this one. Don't let her get away."

The expanse of skin above his scarf turned red again. He craned around, looking absolutely mortified. "Mother . . ."

Tatiana couldn't help the chuckle that filled her throat. "Don't worry, Gilla. I'm not going anywhere."

Her gaze caught his, tangled there. It was more forward than she'd ever been, more pointed. More vulnerable. But when the corner of his lip tugged up, when his blue eyes went a shade darker with feeling, she couldn't bring herself to regret it. It was time to take a few risks. Let him see that if he was interested, she was too.

She suspected the look they shared wasn't lost on his mother, not given the little grin Gilla wore and the way she pulled away a step as Elea and Heidi raced toward Tatiana's building. "Ada," the mother called out, "let's leave them here and go run those errands. And Anders, you needn't rush Heidi home—her mother's busy decorating and Ram isn't home yet, and the boys are all at Dalmar's."

A not-so-subtle hint that Anders and Heidi should not only see them to their door but come in and visit for a while.

Tatiana couldn't help but agree. She reached out to clasp Gilla's hand between hers. "It was so lovely to meet you."

"You're an answer to prayer is what you are." Gilla winked, gave her hand a squeeze, and then turned to give Anders a hug, whispering something in his ear that Tatiana couldn't hear, but which made his cheeks flush yet again.

Poor fellow. Tatiana bided her time while the farewells finished and then gave him a smile she hoped would make up for all the cause for blushing. "If you're not in a rush, we can let the girls play a bit more and visit."

For the first time since they'd come upon his family, his shoulders relaxed. "That sounds perfect."

EIGHT

THOUGH HE'D GOTTEN A GLIMPSE of her flat when he and Heidi came to pick them up earlier, Anders hadn't been able to see enough of it then to know how very much like Tatiana it would feel. Now, though, as he trailed her into the kitchen after leaving their wet boots and snow-dusted coats and hats by the door, he could see that she'd made this place her home in a way he'd never really done with his own flat.

It was in the color choices, all bright and bold. It was in the bookshelves that didn't just have books crammed in like his did, but were artfully arranged, with little knickknacks sharing the display room. It was in the beautiful lamps and lingering scent of cinnamon and spice. It was in the art on her walls.

He froze a step from the kitchen, his gaze latched on the wall of her main room. On the framed watercolor hanging there.

The Lights Watch he'd called it, even penciling the title onto the back when Valdi had commissioned him to paint it for him four years ago. He'd admit that he'd had Tatiana in mind as he painted it, knowing as he did that she'd so recently been living in Hellnar, which he'd painted in silhouette in the middle ground. Above the village danced the northern lights, in shades of green and pink. And there at the bottom, in the foreground, a snowy-white arctic fox paused with one front paw in the air, watching the display, two fox pups tumbling together behind her.

He'd thought Valdi had wanted the piece for himself, to remember the home of his youth. His boss had never once mentioned he'd commissioned it as a gift. If he'd known . . . well, he wouldn't have done anything differently, really. He certainly wouldn't have asked her how she liked it. Still, it was a bit odd, knowing that all this time, the painting he'd done with her in mind was in fact hanging in her home.

Tatiana moved back to his side, apparently noticing his distraction, and followed his gaze. Her lips turned up. "Valdi knew how much I admire your work. I'd confessed that I was saving up to buy a full-sized original but didn't know when I'd have enough, and lo and behold, he gave me that for Christmas that year."

He looked over, down into her beautiful face. "Had you mentioned to me that you wanted a painting, I'd have gladly made you one at no cost."

She sent him a look that he had no trouble deciphering, as often as he earned it from his mother. It said, *Don't be silly,*

Anders. "I wasn't going to go fishing for a gift. Besides, your work is *worth* paying for. I'd have been honored to purchase one."

"I . . ." He didn't know exactly what he meant to say, so he shook his head and let her lead him into the kitchen, their nieces' laughter floating in from wherever they'd gone. Presumably a bedroom, since they weren't in the main room and the flat wasn't that large. When she indicated the table and reached for the kettle, he sank to a seat. "To be quite honest, I'm not accustomed to people I know wanting my artwork."

She set the kettle on the stove with a bit more clatter than he expected of her and spun to face him, eyes wide. "You're kidding, right? I've seen them in the gallery you use—they go for proper money."

"Yes, but . . . they go to *strangers.*" He sighed and pinched the bridge of his nose. "I honestly thought my family had tossed out the paintings I'd done for them. I've never once seen them in their homes, and they never told me they'd hung them in their bedrooms." Obviously he had no cause to venture into his mother's or brothers' private chambers. Laughing a bit at himself, he shook his head again. "I don't know how you did it. Five minutes with my mother, and you've managed to rewrite my entire understanding of my family."

His head was still swirling with it, his equilibrium smashed to pieces. They were beautiful pieces, yes, but still. It was discombobulating to have everything he'd thought he'd known—and mourned—tossed on its head with a few words between Tatiana and Mother.

She *cherished* the painting he'd made of her and Father. So much that she'd hung it where she'd see it first and last thing every day. And had apparently mentioned it to his brothers' wives, if they'd followed suit.

They'd discussed it . . . just not with *him*. And Mother, she . . . she was *proud* of him. Thought him cleverer than the rest of the family. Said she'd always known he'd do great things.

A gentle hand landed on his shoulder, alerting him to the fact that he'd squeezed his eyes shut as he tried to absorb it all. He hadn't seen Tatiana move, but she stood now beside his chair, arm around him to rest that hand on his far shoulder. "You didn't know how proud of you they are?"

Her tone said it was inconceivable. But the inconceivable part was that she'd gotten the truth from his mother and sister so effortlessly.

Or *was* it the truth? Would Mother have lied, just to impress her?

No, that wasn't like his mother at all. She was honest to a fault—blunt and strong and always of the mind that she must be the iron to sharpen her children's iron. She'd never fudge the truth, just as she'd never coddled any of them.

To answer Tatiana, he said, "I . . . didn't. They've never . . . none of them. None of them have ever praised my work. And my brothers, they outright mock me for being an indoors sort, not outside doing manly pursuits like fishing or hunting or farming."

Her hand rubbed over his shoulder. Just a friendly

gesture, meant to give comfort. Right? Yet the small gesture made electricity shoot straight through him, landing in his stomach. He looked over, up into her face. She, too, had said things to his mother she'd never said to him. Did she mean them? Not just that she'd always admired his work—that had nothing to do with *him*, somehow. Not like . . . not like *this*. The fact that she'd said she wasn't going anywhere, intimated that she wasn't opposed to making his mother's assumptions true.

He could get lost in those blue-green eyes of hers. And when she smiled at him like that, in that slow, soft way, his tongue tied in so many knots he'd be lucky to regain use of it by the end of the day.

"Well," she said, "perhaps they're not good at expressing their feelings. It can be difficult—especially if *they* all think you're cleverer than them. That could be a difficult thing for older brothers, don't you think? To see you embracing a world they don't view as their own? Perhaps they even feel like you've rejected the life they've chosen and judge it as inferior."

"Inferior?" Well look at that, he could still speak after all. "They've always made it very clear that mine was the inferior pursuit, to their way of thinking."

She lifted her brows. That was all. Just a graceful arch toward her golden hair. But it was all that was needed to make him hear his own words, and hers again. To combine them with Mother's claim that they were simply teasing him as they did each other.

To remember all the times they harassed each *other* too—and there were endless examples. Those three seemed to approach each day as a competition, and whoever came in last in whatever pursuits they were doing, he earned the mockery of the others.

Strange, though. Whenever he heard them making fun of each other, he could hear the joke in it. He could see, even, that the constant ribbing was what made them so close. Inseparable. Friends as well as brothers.

It had always made him feel more on the outside, since he wasn't part of those daily contests. By his own choice, yes, but . . . but that was because he had *always* come in last. Always felt different. Never thought himself part of their trio. So when they'd turned those cutting words against him, they'd sliced.

"I haven't just misunderstood all these years, have I?" If so, if he'd wasted all this time resenting them and grieving what had actually been there all along . . .

Tatiana sighed and pulled out another of the table's chairs and sat. He missed the arm she'd had around him, but given that she then reached for his hand, he couldn't miss it too long. Her hand felt so small in his. Dainty. Yet her fingers pressed against his with strength and warmth. "Family is so very complicated, isn't it? I daresay there's resentment on their side, just as there is on yours. I imagine they've been frustrated over the years when they simply don't understand your choices. But . . ." She leaned a little closer, eyes agleam. "I also suspect that if we were to eavesdrop on them when you weren't around, you'd find them bragging about their brilliant little brother."

His dubiousness must have shown clearly on his face, given her laugh.

Her fingers squeezed his hand. "I'm serious. Just look at the sagas you've been working on—we have evolved a lot from the days of our Viking ancestors, but the complicated, unshakable family bonds still hold us tight, don't they?"

His lips tugged up a bit at that. Anyone who read the old sagas knew how true that was. Brothers might clash, but they would stand together against an outsider. And yet . . . "Those sagas also highlight our innate preference for the tallest, the strongest, the bravest."

She smiled at him as if he were all those things. Granted, she'd not yet been towered over by Dalmar and Ulric and Ram. "There is more than one way to stand tall, Anders," she said softly. "More than one kind of strength. More than one kind of bravery. I think following the path you know God had prepared for you, when it went against generations of tradition, took far more courage than doing what was expected would have."

Rather than answer, he let her words echo. Let them fill him. Let his thumb stroke over her knuckles, let himself see the pleasure in her eyes that he'd usually try to talk himself into denying was *really* there.

Let himself hope. That she was right. That things with his family could be mended, because they didn't think of him as poorly as he'd always assumed. That she had meant it when she'd said she intended to stay there by his side.

"Could I take you to dinner sometime?" The question

slipped out without any thought. Or second thoughts. Or third, or fourth. Without any stammering or equivocating. Though, of course, he felt the flush crawling up his neck.

She didn't look away from his eyes as she smiled. "Anders, you can take me to dinner *any* time. Though given my current charge . . ." She inclined her head toward the sounds of girlish laughter. "Perhaps for now, you'd let me *make* you dinner?"

"Name the day."

Though she drew her bottom lip between her teeth, it didn't stop her smile from shining. "I don't know. Any of them? All of them? It won't be anything fancy, but I plan to have soups ready, since we'll have long evenings again next week."

Had she really just said *all of them*? His grin felt big enough to crack his cheeks. "I can contribute some fish and bread—my family keeps me well stocked. And perhaps . . . perhaps I could escort you and Elea to your uncle's next weekend, for the Christmas party? I have a car—I don't use it much, but I could drive us. It's a bit too far to walk, I think."

She looked . . . happy. More than happy. Excited. Her eyes danced, and her nod was downright exuberant. "That would be wonderful. Yes. You can't know how long I've . . ." This time, *she* was the one who blushed and stammered to a halt.

Anders lifted her hand, still snug in his, and pressed his lips to her knuckles. "I should have worked up the nerve to ask you sooner. I just . . . you're so beautiful. So bright. I couldn't imagine you'd want to have anything to do with me."

With a chuckle, she rested an elbow on the table and leaned closer, whispering, "We really need to work on that self-esteem of yours, Anders."

"Do we?" He swallowed, remembering the easy way she'd told his mother that she found him handsome.

The kettle whistled, and Tatiana jumped a bit, then laughed at herself as she straightened. She gave his fingers a squeeze and then let go, standing and moving to the stove.

His hand felt cool without hers in it. Empty. But the way she snuck a glance at him over her shoulder made that hope take root. Somehow, it was really happening. His bumbling attempts to help her with her niece had turned into time with *her*, just as he'd dreamed it would. They were . . . they were moving beyond the vague friendship of colleagues. They were making dinner plans. Party plans.

Perhaps, if he didn't stumble over himself too much in the next week, they'd come to be a real couple.

He couldn't think of a finer gift this Christmas.

Gift. He watched her as she poured the boiling water into two mugs and fished tea bags from a tin of them. He'd taken the sketch home with him last night but hadn't yet had time to paint it. And now, seeing the one from Valdi on her wall, he was second-guessing the wisdom of just putting color to the small drawing. It had seemed a fine-enough size when he was just making it for a friend, spurred on by her niece.

Now, though? Something had changed on that walk. Here in this kitchen. He might not know what else to call her just yet, but she wasn't just a friend from work. She was the woman who'd called him handsome. Who'd somehow, with a few words, gotten his mother to express feelings she never had before within his hearing. She was the one who'd put an arm around him, reached for his hand.

She was, without question, the only woman ever to touch his heart in a way that made him dream of forever by her side.

A small, simple drawing wasn't enough. Perhaps he'd match the size of *The Lights Watch*. He even still had a frame to match the one on her wall now. Given the subject matter, her and Elea and books, he knew she'd like it. And the framed painting in the place of honor over her couch did indeed back up her claim of admiring his work.

Still . . . the thought of giving her *only* a painting made doubt wriggle to life in his chest. He couldn't help it. Even if Mother had been telling the truth about where his previous gifts had ended up—he knew she wouldn't lie but still couldn't quite believe it—the fact remained that he'd never actually given a gift of his artwork and watched it be received with anything other than a cool nod and what had struck him as an obligatory "Thank you." The insecurity was too deeply planted to yank out with one tug.

He'd make the bigger painting, to match her current one in size, yes . . . but he'd give her something else, too. A book? She would love *By the Stars at Night* as much as Mother would, and even Ada.

But unlike his family, Tatiana worked at the Story Society. She could get a copy of any book she wanted at the same discount he would use. Giving her one of their own books would be almost insulting.

Although . . . Tandri Ebbisson was reclusive. They knew he lived somewhere in or near Reykjavik, given the post office box address, but he had dodged all questions about the particulars of where he made his home. He would not be hosting book signings, unlike some of their authors.

Through the editorial process over the last year, though, Anders had gotten to know Tandri through their letters and notes. They'd become friends. *Good* friends, even. Somehow it had been easier to open up to a faceless author through words on paper than it ever was in real life, face-to-face. He was fairly certain that, if he sent a few copies of the novel to the author and asked for inscriptions, Ebbisson wouldn't refuse.

He was all but certain no one else would venture such a thing though. Which meant that the copies he sent could well be the only signed copies to be seen. And there had been plenty of talk around the office about how their newest author was such a mystery in some ways. Tatiana would *know* that he went to some trouble to procure the signature. That would make it special, wouldn't it?

A mug of tea appeared before him, and he looked up to see that Tatiana had moved back to the table while he was lost in his schemes. She smiled. "What's going on in that head of yours?"

He found himself returning the smile and, more, felt it go a little mischievous. "Oh no. You're not allowed to ask that question so close to Christmas, Tatiana."

She laughed and opened her mouth, but he never got to hear what clever response she'd offer. Their nieces chose that moment to swoop into the room, and the rest of their shared afternoon was dedicated to their giggles.

NINE

19 DECEMBER 1944

He was getting her a gift. That was what he'd meant on Saturday, Tatiana knew it. Which meant she'd been spending the last two days wracking her brain, trying to think of something to get *him*. It was Tuesday now, and she still had no ideas.

She'd never bought a gift for a man before, other than her family. What in the world was she to give him? With the rationing, there weren't a lot of options, especially since she had only a week's worth of notice, and no time to go shopping.

Leaning back in her wooden desk chair, she lifted her fingers from their places on the typewriter keys and faced facts—she was far too distracted to get any good writing done today. She could still finish the book on time if she skipped this morning . . . so long as she put in a few hours over the holiday.

"Not writing this morning?"

Tatiana jolted and spun on her chair to find Elea standing a few steps behind her, already dressed for the day. Usually she heard her niece get up and move to the bathroom, even when she was involved in her story world. The fact that she'd not heard her today, when all she was doing was fretting, painted far too clear a picture of her mental state. Tatiana summoned a smile . . . and quickly reached to extract the half-filled page from the typewriter so she could slip it into the drawer. "I was trying, but to no avail."

Elea watched her put the page away but then turned toward the kitchen. "Something bothering you?"

She sighed. Her niece really was far too perceptive for a child. It wasn't fair. "Nothing serious. Just debating what I should get Anders for Christmas. I . . . I think he might be giving me something."

Flashing a grin at her over her shoulder, Elea vanished from sight. Though her voice had no trouble finding her. "Oh, he is. And I know what."

"You do not." Tatiana bolted from the chair and hurried to the kitchen. The porridge had been soaking overnight, as usual, and Elea was straining it. "Do you? What is it?"

Elea looked at the table over her shoulder, not toward Tatiana. "Did Skyrgamar eat the *skyr* we left out for him?"

"I know a dodge when I hear one, young lady." But she

could laugh at herself—was she really trying to pry information about a gift from her niece? That was hardly sporting. She motioned to the bowl. "Licked clean, of course. That *skyr* glutton isn't about to let even a drop go to waste."

Seeing Elea's grin was definitely worth the late-night snack she hadn't really wanted. Tatiana had conspired with several other parents and grandparents in the building to stage some door slamming early Monday morning too, to convince all the children that Hurthaskellir, known for his too-exuberant entrances and exits, had been in the building.

"I bet if we look toward the mountains, we'll see his sledding tracks too." She put the bowl in the sink and then turned the water on to rinse the grains while Elea fetched the pot from its cupboard. This had become their routine over the last few days. They'd get the porridge on and then, while it was simmering, go check the shoes in the windowsill.

Still, she couldn't help one more try. "I don't expect you to tell me what he's getting me, but . . . you could help me pick something out for him. Something . . . equal."

Elea held the pot while Tatiana poured the wet grains into it, then covered them with water and added a pinch of salt. "I'll give you *one* hint—he's not *getting* you anything."

"Emphasis on *getting*, I see." The only other options she could think of were that he was taking her somewhere or making her something.

She let out a huff of breath. When it came to crafting, she had no particular skills. She was a horror with a crochet hook or knitting needles, and she could sew only enough to get by, not enough to whip up a gift for a special someone in less than a week. She was no artist, and though she could bake reasonably well, she didn't think a plate of cookies and leaf bread would be all that special to him, given that his family kept him well supplied.

"You should write him a story," Elea said as she carefully slid the pot onto the stove. "He likes stories better than *anything*."

Tatiana smiled and set the kitchen timer for twenty minutes. "He's in the right profession, then. But I don't think—"

"Why not? I bet your stories are great. You probably have some in that drawer of yours that you could use." Eyes lighting, she turned to face Tatiana. "We could turn one into a real book! We did that in school a few months ago. We wrote poems and illustrated them and then sewed them into a book. Teacher gave us cardboard, and we each found fabric from our mothers' scrap bins and pasted it over the cardboard to make the covers. Just like a real book!"

"That sounds lovely." And given her laughable skills with scissors and glue, if she tried such a thing, it would probably look like a seven-year-old had done it too. "I'll keep the idea in mind."

Elea glared at her a moment, then spun for the kitchen's exit. "I know what that means. It means you don't think it's a good idea."

"I think it's a great idea," Tatiana said, scurrying after her. "I just doubt my own ability to make it into a worthwhile gift."

Elea turned to her shoe—and let out a gasp as she pulled out the handle with the rolling slicer. "A leaf bread iron! Yay, we can make it after all!"

Tatiana had been making do with a knife to cut the intricate pattern since she moved to the city, but as they'd plotted out their baking on Sunday, Elea had been appalled at the idea of freehanding it. And given Tatiana's admittedly lacking artistic skills, it was a fair point. She'd sent some money with one of the secretaries who left for lunch yesterday and had her pick one up for her.

Now she grinned. "Amazing how those Yule Lads know just what we need, isn't it?" She reached into her own shoe and feigned surprise. "And cookie cutters too! We will be all set for our baking."

Elea gave her a quick hug and then dashed toward the phone. "I'm going to call Mamma and tell her."

The calls had gotten easier on the girl as the days went by, and Tatiana was glad of it. Glad to see her looking forward to the moments with her parents on the phone instead of crying at the sound of the voices that were too far away. "All right. I'm going to go down and collect yesterday's post. I forgot last night."

"Because *Anders* was with us," her niece taunted with a laugh. She picked up the receiver and dialed the exchange, an old hand at it by now.

Tatiana grabbed a discarded piece of paper from the end table, balled it up, and lobbed it at Elea's head, earning her more laughter.

Though she wasn't wrong. It was indeed Anders's presence that had made her completely forget her usual stop at the letter boxes in the lobby.

And as she pulled out the parcel wrapped in brown paper with Anders's own handwriting on the front, she thanked the Lord above that she hadn't paused here last night with him beside her . . . and wondered if she'd been a fool to have Tandri Ebbisson's mail forwarded to her here from the post-box. When she'd put in the order two months ago, it had seemed a time-saving step with no possible repercussions.

But now? *Idiot!* It wasn't just that Anders could get a glimpse of her pseudonym, but that Elea very easily could, and then what? She could explain to her niece and swear her to secrecy . . . but that was hardly fair to the girl. How could she ask her to keep a secret from her parents?

Thankfully, Elea was still chatting happily on the phone when Tatiana regained her flat. They set a ten-minute limit each day, since it was long-distance, and Elea had no doubt checked the clock as they were connected. By Tatiana's guess, there were probably six or seven minutes left, at least.

Plenty of time. She slipped into the bedroom and closed the door, then quickly unwrapped the parcel and stashed the incriminating paper in the bottom of her wastebasket. But then she frowned. It was . . . copies of her book. But that made no sense. He'd already sent her her author copies, all but one of which she'd hidden away. Why would he send her three more?

A note was tucked into the topmost one, its edge just barely visible. She tugged it out, exhaling slowly as she read.

Tandri,

I do hope this isn't too presumptuous—but as I've been debating what gifts to give some of my favorite people, I've decided that your book is sure to bring them the smiles that I love to see on their faces. Could I trouble you for your signature on these? I've included return postage, tucked into the final book. If you're willing, please make one out to Gilla (my mother), Ada (my sister), and Tatiana (a very special someone) with whatever message you think is best. They'll be delighted, I know. To prove myself of pure motivations here and not just trying to leverage our acquaintance, you'll note that I restrained myself and didn't include my own copy to be made out to me. If, however, this is overstepping, you can of course just return the books unsigned.

May your Christmas be filled with joy.

Your friend,
Anders

Tatiana sank onto the edge of her bed, thoughts too muddled to make sense of them at first. There was the pleasure, to be sure—he thought so highly of her book that he wanted to give it as gifts to his mother and sister! Then . . . *her*. He'd called her "a very special someone." And wanted to give her a signed copy of her own book.

Gracious, but this was ridiculous, wasn't it? She couldn't . . . she couldn't just sign a book to herself, that would be absurd.

She had to tell him.

She couldn't just *tell* him.

She should . . . do . . . something. But what?

And wait, Elea had said he wasn't "getting" her something, but wasn't this exactly that? He was not only getting her a book—which she could have gotten herself easily enough—but getting it signed—which he would assume she *couldn't* so easily get for herself.

It was thoughtful. And if he were to present her with any *other* book signed by its reclusive author, she'd be over the moon with delight.

But her own? Maybe she should just do it, to avoid the question. Sign it and send it back and then . . . feign surprise and delight? She didn't know if she was so good an actress.

From beyond her door, she could hear Elea singing a verse of one of her favorite Christmas songs, as she did each day before saying goodbye. Which meant Tatiana had no time to actually sort this out now. She dropped to her knees on the floor, pulled out one of the lidded boxes she stored under the bed and in which she kept correspondence, and dropped the books and note inside.

She'd deal with them later. Tonight, after Anders had once more joined them for soup and bread and the fish he'd promised to bring with him. After he'd gone and Elea was preparing for bed, she'd pull it back out, take the whole box out to her desk. Elea was accustomed to her tending her correspondence in the evenings, after she'd tucked her in. She'd certainly sign the ones for his mother and sister, using the signature that she'd practiced and used on the notes she sent to him with her edited pages. She'd rewrap them and use the postage he'd included, then just drop the package in a letter box for pickup. Easy enough.

Except for that third copy.

Bother. *Later*, she'd sort out what to do about that later. For now she stashed the box back under her bed and emerged again from her bedroom just as Elea was saying goodbye. The porridge still had a few minutes to cook, so Tatiana edged past her niece toward the bathroom to take the rollers from her hair. "How's everything at home?"

"Good." Elea leaned into the open doorway and watched her take out the rollers, releasing her hair into curls. "Mamma says Pabbi got a good report from the doctor yesterday and should be ready to go back out on the boat after Christmas. And he can walk a little now, just not for long. And Mamma says the baby's been kicking like crazy and bruising her insides."

Tatiana smiled. Kicking was good. Kicking meant *life* and health and hope. "Good indeed! Did you tell her that Skyrgamur brought us a leaf bread iron?"

"Of course. And I told her that we had a very special guest for dinner last night, and that he's coming again tonight."

At the gloating note in her niece's voice, Tatiana's hands paused, and she sent a narrowed-eyed gaze to the little imp. "And what exactly did you tell her about Anders?"

Elea giggled. "That he can't stop looking at you and trips over his own feet whenever you're near, and that you think he's *so* handsome and clever and that his mother invited us over for Christmas Eve."

Resuming her roller removing, Tatiana hummed. "I suppose all of that is true."

"And that I hope you get married so that Heidi and I will be cousins." She paused, frowned. "Would that make us cousins? If my aunt and her uncle are married?"

"Close enough, I'd think." She sent a wink Elea's way. "But let's not get ahead of ourselves, my little Yule Lass. We haven't even had an official date."

"But you've been working together for*ever*! You're already friends, and his mother likes you. Heidi said her *ommu* is always trying to find girls to set him up with, but she always says, 'No, no, she's not right for my Anders. My Anders needs a *clever* girl.'"

At the imitation of Gilla—rather good for a seven-year-old, based on their single meeting, anyway—Tatiana cracked a smile. "Does she now?"

"That's what Heidi said. And I said you're as clever as you are pretty, so it's no wonder he likes you, and I'm glad her *ommu* likes you too." She wrinkled her nose. "Ommu Margret still says mean things about Mamma sometimes, when she thinks I'm not listening."

At that, Tatiana spun to face her niece, eyes wide. "I hope you didn't tell your mother that." Ari was well aware that she hadn't been Margret's first choice for Gunnar, but one would think that after nearly nine years of marriage, Margret would have gotten over her hopes that he'd have chosen her best friend's daughter.

Elea shook her head, expression earnest. "I'd never hurt Mamma's feelings like that." She paused, pursed her lips. "I told Pabbi some of the things she'd said though. His mouth went all tight and flat and he stomped out the door, saying he was going to pay her a visit. She hasn't said anything since then. Least, not that I've heard."

Good. If Tatiana knew Gunnar at all, he'd given his mother an earful and . . . *hmm*. "When was that?"

"A couple months ago. Ommu Margret's been awful busy since then. I've barely seen her."

Another reason, then, that they'd asked Tatiana to take Elea rather than getting help from the grandparents. She pulled the last roller out, ran her brush through the curls to loosen them, and pinned back the sides. Then she turned to Elea and spun her finger in a circle.

Elea obediently spun around, holding out a hand. Tatiana placed the ribbons that would match today's dress in her palm and brushed out her silken hair. "You did the right thing, telling your *pabbi*."

"I know," she said easily. "I love Ommu, but it's not right, the things she said about Mamma. Besides, Mamma's getting better now. This baby . . . this baby's going to be fine, and

Mamma's going to be fine, and she's not going to be so sad anymore."

Tatiana used the end of a comb to part Elea's hair down the middle, gathered the left side and draped it over her shoulder to keep it out of the way, and started the first braid on the right side. "I pray you're right," she said. She didn't want to say that, even if the baby was healthy—which, pray God, he or she would be—that didn't mean Ari's sorrow would go away. Tatiana was the last of her friends to get married, which meant she'd had plenty of opportunity to attend weddings and then *ooh* and *aah* over cute little newborns, and Ari wasn't the only young woman who struggled with feeling blue in the months following a birth.

"I am." Elea's tone said so much more than her words. That she *needed* to be right, that she had to believe. But also that she *did* believe. "You should have heard her when I told her about Anders. She laughed and clapped, and I could *hear* her smiling, Aunt Tatta. I haven't heard her so happy in . . . a long time. She's getting better. I know she is."

Tatiana paused her braiding long enough to lean down and drop a kiss to the top of Elea's head. "Then I believe you. You know your mother better than anyone but your *pabbi* does, I think."

"She said she wants to talk to you tomorrow." A tease, now, in her voice. "I think she wants all the juicy details."

Tatiana chuckled, finished off the braid, and reached for one of the ribbons to tie around the end. "I'll be sure to exaggerate every detail for her."

"I don't think you have to. I think Anders has liked you for a long, long time. I think now that he knows you like him, he's going to take his mother's advice and never let you go."

Tatiana moved to the left side, not even trying to keep the smile from her lips. "I hope you're right. I've liked him for a long, long time too."

Her niece grinned. "It's a good thing I came to visit, isn't it? Otherwise, who knows if he ever would have said a thing!"

"A very excellent point." But those books she'd hidden under her bed all but taunted her, reminding her that she couldn't exactly build a good relationship on a foundation of secrets. She had to tell him.

Soon.

Somehow.

TEN

20 DECEMBER 1944

Anders lifted Elea up, hands about her waist, and held her steady while she fastened the garland over the curtain rods. "And *that*," he said, sliding sideways so she could hook the greenery in the middle, then again on the other end, "is why we must be sure to get all the decorations up before Gluggagaegir comes tonight. He would be very disappointed if he peeked in the window and didn't see colorful things! So disappointed, he'd forget to leave you your gift and would mope his way back to his boring gray cave."

Elea fastened the end and grinned at him over her shoulder. "Then it's a good thing we got all the book orders sent out this morning, so we had time this evening."

"A good thing indeed." And not only for the sake of the

decorations—tomorrow would be Thursday, December 21. There were only a few days of post runs left before Christmas, and Valdi had led them all in a prayer as they sent out the last of the orders that they would reach their recipients—all in Reykjavik—in time. They *should*, if the postal workers made no mistakes and were as dedicated as the staff in the warehouse had been. Most of them should arrive tomorrow, Friday at the latest.

It made him smile every time he thought about it—every household in Iceland, opening books for Christmas. Every family exclaiming, sharing, trading, reading. They were a storytelling people—from the ancient epics to the medieval sagas to the books being written today. From the fish stories his brothers told to the exaggerated schoolyard tales of his nephews and nieces. From his own children's stories to the brilliant novels he helped edit.

He lowered Elea back to the ground and said another prayer for another delivery—that when he got back to his flat tonight, there'd be a package from Tandri waiting for him. He'd given his home address for the return, unlike their usual correspondence, which all went through the Story Society. But he couldn't risk having part of Tatiana's gift delivered there, not with how often she was the one to distribute the mail. Not that she'd know what was in it, but what if she guessed?

No, better to keep the secret.

He sneaked a glance at Tatiana, who was fitting the dowel-rod branches of her homemade Christmas tree into their holes. Hers was about the same size as his, small enough to sit on a tabletop, easy to take apart and store away in a closet or under a bed the rest of the year. "My mother said to be sure and tell you she's getting a real pine tree this year. She seems to think that will be incentive to come."

Oh, when she smiled at him like that, sly and teasing, it made his heart turn cartwheels. "That *is* good incentive. We've never had a real pine tree, as expensive as they are to import. I was hoping we could find some juniper boughs or heather to drape over the rods to make branches though."

"Will you come over early on Saturday and help us get the decorations on the tree?" Elea moved over to the boxes of ornaments which were, as per tradition, still packed up. They may put their trees together earlier, given that it usually required some patience to fit all the rods into their holes or situate whatever other handcrafted "tree" had been devised, but no one ever adorned those branches until the twenty-third. "Then we can go to Uncle Valdi's party."

"That sounds like a delightful plan." He nearly tacked on *if it's all right with your aunt*, but bit his tongue. Still, he glanced again at Tatiana, and he could have sworn she'd heard the silent addition anyway, given the twinkle in her eyes.

Last night, when Elea had asked him to join their decorating party, he *had* said it, and Tatiana had sighed, reached for his hands, and said, "Anders, repeat after me. *Tatiana always wants me to come over. I don't need to ask her if it's all right to accept the invitations.*"

Instead, he'd frowned, even as his fingers gripped hers. "You'll get tired of me."

Her eyes had positively gleamed, and she'd leaned close enough that Elea had begun giggling. "That's not going to happen," she'd said, voice low. Husky. The kind of whisper that had made his gaze drop to her red-painted lips.

To be sure he was hearing her right, he'd told himself.

Because he wanted to kiss her, he admitted to himself in turn, after hearing how that bald-faced lie clanged around in his conscience.

He hadn't, of course, not with the giggling audience. And, well . . . perhaps too because he hadn't dared to. As long as they were simply sharing dinners and occasionally holding hands, he could convince himself that he hadn't ruined anything yet.

But once he kissed her, everything would change. They wouldn't just be friends. They *couldn't* just be friends. Which meant that when he messed everything up somehow or she grew bored of him, they couldn't *again* be friends. Right now, if she decided after her niece went home that his main charm had been as half of a babysitting team, well . . . he'd be crushed, of course, but they could just go back to normal. Pleasantries in the corridors and him eavesdropping on her conversations with Valdi at the coffeepot or with Helga in his own office.

Blast, but he was pathetic. It would be a wonder if she *didn't* cut him loose before Christmas even came.

"Anders." Her voice was a laugh, a chide.

He sighed. "I didn't say it."

"You were *thinking* it. I could hear you all the way over here." She picked up another green-painted dowel. And grinned. "You're lucky I find your insecurities so adorable."

Adorable? He'd been called many things in life, but never that. Well, perhaps when he was a baby. He had been an extraordinarily adorable baby—he'd seen the photographs, it couldn't be denied. But not since his curls had straightened, for sure.

Naturally, heat crept up his throat, and when she laughed, he sighed. "You're going to be the death of me. Death by blushing. Which is so very unheroic that my brothers will compose an un-saga to be sure people will be able to make fun of me for generations to come."

She abandoned her tree, moved over to his side, stretched up on her tiptoes, and pressed her lips to his too-warm cheek. "I like your blushing too," she whispered in his ear.

"Murderer," he muttered as his cheeks flamed hotter. But he smiled. Hard not to, when she stood so close and looked up at him as if . . . well, as if she meant it.

Part of him whispered that she wouldn't for long. She'd come to Mother's on Christmas Eve and see his brothers, see all he wasn't, and decide she'd hold out for another strapping, hero-worthy man. She'd meet someone smarter. Richer. More accomplished. A prince of a man, exactly as she deserved.

But another part told him to hold on tight. Not let her go. Fight for her, however he had to. Because she seemed to be that rare kind of person—one who saw him, understood him, and wanted to know him better instead of turning away.

She moved back to her tree, which freed his mind up enough to notice that Elea stood there grinning, another evergreen bough in her arms. "One more window," the little one said.

"Well, we'd better get to it then. Don't want to disappoint Gluggagaegir."

They soon had the decorating done, and though Tatiana insisted he didn't need to hurry off . . . in fact, he did. He still had work to do on her painting. So he said his farewells, made a mental note to buy enough juniper boughs for both his own tree and hers tomorrow on his way to work, and hurried home.

It only took ten minutes to walk from her flat to his, and it made him wonder why they hadn't been all the time running into each other at the shops in addition to seeing each other at work. But they each had their separate routines, he supposed, and they hadn't often overlapped.

No matter. Now he knew each turn to take him to her home and had an open invitation to join her for dinner, which still flabbergasted him.

How could he possibly be so fortunate?

Or maybe not *so* fortunate. When he opened his own door after gathering his post—there was a package from Tandri, praise the Lord—he saw a light on that he'd turned out that morning and smelled fish frying. He toed off his shoes and deposited his things in their places as Enja darted out of his bedroom to come give his legs a purring cuddle in welcome, wondering which of his brothers had let himself in this time. It wouldn't be Mother cooking—she'd known he was eating at Tatiana's again.

As for why one of his brothers—Dalmar, he saw as he moved toward the kitchen with the cat in his arms—was *cooking* . . . "This is a first."

Ulric was the tallest by an inch, but Dalmar didn't need that extra inch to come across as a giant. He was still six foot five, broad enough to fill the doorframes he had to duck through, and solid muscle from his days spent hauling gear. He looked over his shoulder in a silent greeting.

Well, *greeting* would be stretching the meaning of the word. But in acknowledgment, anyway.

Anders leaned into the doorframe, letting Enja jump down when she squirmed for freedom. "I do thank you for making me dinner, but I've already eaten." Which was good, because that fish looked more than a little burnt on one side. He'd have a fine time getting *that* reek out in a season when he couldn't exactly open the windows.

Even Enja agreed—she ran back out of the kitchen instead of leaping onto the counter to investigate the fish, one of her favorite treats.

Dalmar grunted. "Not for you."

"I . . . see." Except he didn't. "And you're cooking your own dinner, presumably, in my kitchen . . . why?"

His brother's shoulders bunched up. "Because Kristin told me I wasn't welcome to eat at my *own* home, and our mother took her side, and I wasn't about to go to Ulric's or Ram's and have them harangue me."

Kristin had . . . ? Anders moved into the kitchen and elbowed his brother aside. "Let me help. You in a kitchen is about as natural as a polar bear in the tropics." He risked a glance up the five inches to his brother's face. "Want to talk about it?"

He wouldn't. He never did. Dalmar wasn't the talking kind—he was the doing kind.

Which was why Anders nearly dropped the spatula when his brother sagged against the workbench and let out a long sigh. "I really put my foot in it this time."

Play it cool, he told himself. *Don't scare him away.* He turned down the heat on the stove—no wonder one side had burned, but no way had it cooked through yet—and kept his gaze on the pan instead of Dalmar's face. "What happened?"

Even so, he caught his brother's wince in his peripheral vision. "Garri, he . . . he came home from school—last day before break, you know—all excited. The school had been holding a contest. Short stories—Christmas stories. His won. Not just his class or his grade, but out of the whole school."

Well he couldn't not look over at that news, any more than he could restrain his smile. "That's wonderful! He must have been so proud of himself."

Dalmar, he couldn't help but notice, winced again. "Yeah . . . he was. And his mother was." He fell silent.

It said plenty. Anders gusted out a breath. "Dalmar. What did you say?"

His brother straightened, contrition turning into anger on his face. Ah, *this* was the Dalmar he knew. He waved a brawny arm. "What was I *supposed* to say? The boy is ten years old—ten! And already, he's too smart, too clever. Ten years old, and I don't know what he's talking about half the time. Bad enough I have to feel the idiot around *you*, but my own boy?"

"Wait, you . . . ?" Anders turned the stove down a bit more so that he could turn to face Dalmar fully. "You are not an *idiot*, you idiot." Yes, he heard himself. "Other than when you act this way. Where do you think Garri got his intelligence?"

"From *you*!" He roared it like an accusation.

Not that it was *that* sort of accusation. Anders rolled his eyes. "We're a clever family—all of us. We just focus it on different things. I like words. Ulric likes numbers. Ram likes nature. You like machines. If you don't understand what I say half the time, we're even. When you ramble on about engines, my eyes glaze over. So stop being a coward and let your son be who he wants to be."

Dalmar went still. Well, other than that pulsing vein in his temple. "What did you just call me?"

Anders smiled, even though he knew very well it would infuriate his brother. Always had, always would. "If you don't want to be called a coward, stop acting like one. You can brave the fiercest storm, the wiliest rival—you don't even cower at the thought of German U-boats! But the thought of your son being more like me than you? That terrifies you." He added a dollop of butter to the pan and then put on the lid. Faced the giant down. Lifted his chin. "Is it such a bad thing, Dal? To be like me? Do you hate me so much?"

He expected a roar. A sneer. An insult. Instead, his brother deflated, going so far as to sink onto one of the chairs that he always dwarfed. "Now *you're* being an idiot. I'm prouder of you than—I don't know. You'd have the words, but I don't, and that's the irony of the thing."

"See there?" He pointed. "You know what irony is. Three points. Idiots wouldn't know that."

Was that actually a breath of laughter that puffed from his lips, or another grunt? Hard to tell, sometimes, with Dalmar. He reached up and rubbed at that bulging vein in his temple. "I don't know how to be a father to him." His voice had gone soft, low, uncertain. "Apparently I've done a lousy-enough job being a brother to you, if you honestly think I don't crow over your every book to everyone I know. The teasing, the prodding, the insults—those work with Ul and Ram. They work with Johann and Hans," he said of Garri's younger brothers. "I know how to talk to them about the things they care about. But Garri? He comes home talking about books I've never even heard of. About scientific stuff that means nothing to me. About *art*."

On another day, in another conversation, the way he sneered *art* would have made Anders bristle. But just now, it made him choke on a laugh. "Not *art*. The horror."

Dalmar crossed beefy arms over his chest. And glared. "And Mother says you don't play with insults like the rest of us."

His lips twitched. "I lean more to the sarcastic. It's never been her forte. She excels at the outright insult and has even honed her skill at the more subtle art of the backhanded insult. But sarcasm . . . she's never gained a taste for it."

"You were adopted," Dalmar grunted.

Anders snorted at the decades-old taunt. "I'm the spitting image of Father."

Dalmar's mouth twitched much like Anders's had just done. "He was adopted too."

He laughed—he couldn't help it. Then he sighed and leaned against the workbench. "Dal—you don't have to understand everything he likes. You don't have to understand *him*. You just have to accept him. Accept that he can love you and look up to you without wanting to follow in your footsteps. I promise you, that boy doesn't think you're an idiot. What he thinks you are is a hero—the one person in the world he most wants to please, and the one person he fears he never will."

Heaving a sigh, Dalmar leaned forward until he'd rested his elbows on his knees, then dropped his head into his hands. He sat that way for a long moment, and Anders said nothing. Just let him think. When the aroma of butter-seared fish met his nose, he turned around, checked on the food, and turned off the stove.

He put the least-burnt pieces onto a plate and set it on the table in front of Dalmar. His brother straightened, but he didn't turn toward the plate. "I don't think . . . I don't think you know what it feels like, to have someone you love so much, someone you have such hopes for, say that what you do, what you've chosen, who you *are* isn't good enough."

Anders frowned. "I know *exactly* how that feels."

But his brother was shaking his head. "You don't. You can't. Our family—we've always been fishermen, Anders. All of us. Every grandfather, every uncle, every cousin, every brother. Until *you*. You had to go to university. You had to write books. You had to draw and paint and . . . and don't you see what that felt like to the rest of us? Like you were saying the lives we'd all lived for generations weren't good enough for you. You needed *more*."

His throat went tight. "Not more—just different. Don't you think it was torture for me, feeling as though I never fit in? That no matter how I tried, I couldn't conform myself to the mold I should have fit?" He got a glass down from the cupboard and pulled the bottle of milk from the icebox—Dalmar always liked milk with his dinner. "I *wanted* to be good at the same things the rest of you were. I *wanted* to make you all proud, not be the runt of the litter you were ashamed to even claim."

"We were never ashamed of you." Dalmar let his hand fall to the table, rattling the plate.

Anders put the glass beside it and fished cutlery from the drawer. "You hung a sign around my neck when I was six that said *Brother for Sale*."

Another twitch of his lips. "That was nothing personal, I did it to Ul and Ram too. As if any of the neighbors would take them. You, now—I had a couple good offers. Aron Frithricksson would have traded me his new wagon for you, so you could help him with his schoolwork."

Having nothing else to occupy his hands, Anders sat in the other chair, laughing. "Aron—*he* was an idiot."

"And I, loving brother that I am, decided not to make the deal. See? You owe me." He picked up the fork but just stared at his half-burned dinner. "It's hard, Anders. Working day in and day out, just finally making enough to buy a few luxuries now that the Americans are importing our catches. While you sit at a desk and just . . . be *smart* all day, and make more than all of us combined. It's hard not to feel like I'm letting down our mother, Kristin, the children."

"Dalmar—"

"Then Garri." Dalmar shook his head. "He's so like you. And I look at him, and I think, *He got it. My brother got it. Why didn't I? Why did it just . . . pass right through me? To him?* And I worry that I won't be able to do right by him. I can't send him to university, Anders, there's no way. All I have to offer him is the fishing boat. But it's not going to be good enough for him. I know it's not, and . . ."

And that would hurt. Just like feeling forced into a life that didn't fit hurt. Anders drew in a long breath. "Dalmar, you're exactly who you were meant to be. And God gave you the children he did because he knew he could trust you to be their father. You don't need to give more than you're able. All you need to do is encourage Garri to be who God created *him* to be. Perhaps he'll decide to run the boat—or perhaps he'll leave it to Johann and Hans and try something different. If he wants to go to university, he can get scholarships, like I did. Just . . . don't let him go, thinking you're not proud of him. Don't let him feel like a failure, like you only value the things he's not good at."

Dalmar cut a bite of fish with his fork but didn't raise it to his lips. "What if I try . . . and still I can't be what he needs? What then?"

"All he needs is for you to try." Anders set his hand down beside his brother's. Solidarity, even if they were so very different. "Eat your fish, brother. Then go home and apologize to your wife for being an idiot and tell your son you're proud of him. Ask to read his story. Joke, if you want to, about how he might need to define any words you don't know. Let him feel clever. *Make* him feel clever. That's the only gift he's ever going to need from you."

His brother nodded. Took a bite, chewed, swallowed. For a minute, they were otherwise silent. Then Dalmar started to look like Dalmar again. The uncertainty faded away, and the prankster reemerged. "You're not half bad at this parenting thing. And Mother says you're bringing a girl with you to Christmas Eve?" He reached a foot over and nudged Anders's shin. "Finally find a woman to make you abandon your bachelor ways?"

Anders blinked. "Don't you mean 'a woman who can stand you' or 'a woman desperate enough to give you a chance'?"

But Dalmar nodded beyond him. "That her?"

Anders spun, as if he *really* thought Tatiana had followed him home and somehow snuck in without him noticing. But then he saw what Dalmar had been motioning toward—the paper on his easel, with her and Elea and the books and the background all sketched out, and the background colors filled in. He relaxed. "It is. And her niece."

"She's pretty. Mother said she was, but she was so excited, I didn't know if I should believe her. She's convinced this is the girl you're going to marry." Dalmar chuckled. "If that look on your face is any indication, I think she's right."

No point trying to school his features now, he supposed. Anders sighed. "I hope so. Tatiana is . . . she's . . . I . . ."

Dalmar grinned. "If she's rendered you speechless, she *must* be something."

He returned the grin. "She really is." Heaven knew she'd been rendering him speechless since he first met her.

"Good. High time you settle down. And I hope you have a son just like me, and one like Ram, and one like Ul—"

"So my own children can beat me up?" But the smile didn't fade. "I'd count myself blessed, Dal."

Dalmar made short work of the fish, then rose to put the plate in the sink. Asking him to wash it was clearly a bridge too far, so Anders just followed him back out to the door.

"If Kristin's still mad, I might be back. Save a place on the couch for me."

"It's yours, but you won't need it." Dalmar loved his wife too much to let the day end with this between them. And she was crazy about him. Painting them had been easy, the way they always leaned into each other.

Which made his lips purse. "Do you remember that painting I did of the two of you?"

Dalmar blinked. "Hard to forget, given that it's staring at me from the foot of my bed."

A little thrill went through him. "You . . . you never told me what you did with it. I never saw it out. I thought . . ."

Dalmar's brows rose. "You thought what?"

"I don't know. That you stashed it in the attic or threw it out. You barely reacted when you opened it. Kristin didn't either."

Dalmar shrugged into his coat. "Maybe *you're* the idiot. We were choked up, you fool. Couldn't speak around it. And it's . . . it's not the sort of thing we just *say*."

Anders's chest felt warm. Full. "We could, you know."

His brother shot him a look. And reached for the door. "You know that thing about letting people be who they are?"

Anders grinned. "Dal?"

"What?"

"Why do you always say no when I ask if you want a copy of my latest book?"

His brother squared his shoulders. And opened the door. "Because I *buy* them, you numbskull. To support you. We all do."

Confusion warred with the glow. "I've never seen them with your children's books. Anyone's." And heaven knew he was acquainted with each and every shelf, as often as he read to his nieces and nephews.

Dalmar looked at him like he really was an idiot. "You think we'd put them there to be torn up and worn out? They're with the family Bibles."

With the . . . heirlooms?

Dalmar rolled his eyes. "Good night, Anders. See you on Christmas Eve."

"Night." He stood there until his brother's footsteps faded down the stairs. Then he turned and smiled at the half-painted Jolabokaflod. It seemed this Christmas was one of miracles.

The smile lasted until he picked up the post he'd deposited by the door and unwrapped the books from Tandri. Then he read the note.

Anders,

Of course I'd be pleased to sign these books for you and your mother and sister! You ought to know by now that it's no presumption. As I count my blessings in these last few weeks of the year, I'm so grateful to number you as one of my friends. Thank you again for all the hard work you put into my story. The next one is nearly finished, and I should have it to you on time.

I hope you and your family have a beautiful Christmas.

Tandri

His smile faded. Wait . . . no. He set the note aside and flipped open the first book—signed to Gilla. The next—to Ada. The third . . . he winced. To *him*. "No," he moaned. He'd *known* he shouldn't have included that jest about signing one to him. No doubt when sitting down to sign them, Tandri had been thinking most about that and had then just skimmed and grabbed the first two names he'd listed.

He sighed and set the three books on his desk. There wasn't time enough to send him another to sign and get it back before Christmas Eve. So . . . he'd just have to hope that Elea was right, and the painting would be a good-enough gift.

ELEVEN

23 DECEMBER 1944

On Friday, Gattathefur the Door Sniffer came, so they had to make sure the flat was tidy, no stinky socks left in the laundry to scare the big-nosed troll away. Tatiana and Elea went to work at the normal hour, which felt so luxurious that Tatiana still got up early and spent the time writing, her fingers flying as the final chapters of the story clicked into place. Anders's brothers sent fresh fish again for dinner, and it took forever to get Elea to settle into bed after he left, so excited was she for the Christmas Party at Uncle Valdi's the next day.

Saturday dawned cold and snowy, but that was no surprise on December 23. They exclaimed over Ketkrokur the Meat Hook eating *all* the sausage they'd left out for him (it was currently hidden in her freezer, because Tatiana wasn't about to try to eat that much sausage before bed, but Elea had counted the pieces before they put them out for him) and prepared the kitchen for baking.

Tatiana got the lamb fat into her deep pot and set it to heating while Elea, with the help of a chair, pulled out the saved-up rations of flour and sugar. They laughed as they mixed the dough for the leaf bread, rolled it out as thin as they could get it, and Elea took the lead using their new iron to cut decorative designs. Leaves here, snowflakes there. Tatiana handled lowering the dough into the bubbling fat and lifting it again on a slotted spoon soon after, the scent of crisp fried dough filling the kitchen.

They baked their cookies and even had enough sugar left over to make a small batch of icing for decorating them.

Then they began looking at the clock. Anders had promised to come over at three, so they'd have enough time to decorate the tree and then for the girls to get ready. The party began at six, but it would take at least twenty minutes to drive to Valdi's house . . . possibly more like thirty, depending on how much snow fell today.

"Did you decide what to get him?" Elea asked at two thirty, as they scraped the bits of flour and dough and sugar off the table. They'd been careful, so there wasn't much waste to clean up.

Tatiana sighed and held the rubbish bin for Elea to scrape the bits into. She'd taken her lunch hour yesterday to go shopping—Helga and Anders had insisted they'd watch Elea through lunch, when she'd said she hadn't yet gotten anything for Valdi or his family. She'd found earrings for Camilla, a beautiful scarf for Beta, even a lovely fountain pen for Valdi, since his had seen better days.

But nothing she saw in the sparsely stocked shops looked right for Anders. Nothing said, *I know you and want to know you more*. Nothing said, *I want this to be the beginning of forever*.

It had been all she could do to shake off the frustration and enjoy their evening together. But as she'd lain in bed last night, mind churning not only over the gift dilemma and the recent days, but also the ending to her novel, she realized Elea had been right all along.

"I decided to take your advice."

Her niece grinned. "You're writing him a story?" Elea clapped. "Yay! Is that what you were working on yesterday?"

Throat too tight suddenly for words, Tatiana nodded.

A knock on the door silenced any further questions, which suited her fine. It was early to be Anders . . . yet somehow she wasn't surprised to open the door and find him there, a sheepish grin on his face and juniper boughs in his arms.

"I'm early, I know," he said, coming in when she stepped aside for him. "But I didn't know how far I'd have to drive to find these so I gave myself far too much time, as it turned out."

She breathed in the fresh scent, eyes going wide. "I thought it was a lost cause!" They'd both looked at the usual vendors the last two days, but neither had found either juniper or heather. She'd resigned herself to a bare-limbed dowel-rod tree this year.

She ought to have known Anders wouldn't accept that answer. "You're my hero!"

He shook his head, but the grin didn't leave his face. "Hardly an epic feat."

"It is to me." To prove it, she leaned up to kiss his cheek, as she'd taken to doing whenever she could find an excuse, just to see the way his eyes lit. And the way he'd glance at her lips.

One of these days, he'd kiss her. Or if he dragged his feet about it much longer, then she'd just take matters into her own hands. A thought that had her grinning as Elea dashed up to take some of the boughs from him.

Between the three of them, they soon had the fresh greenery fastened to the wooden rods.

"What's your tree like at home?" Anders asked Elea as he carried the boxes of ornaments from where Tatiana had stashed them beside the sofa to the end table that now held the fragrant tree.

"Big!" Elea stretched her arms upward, but she couldn't get high enough. "As tall as you, at least. My *pabbi* made it for Mamma their first Christmas together, before I was born. It's a lot like Aunt Tatta's—all wooden rods painted green. Just bigger."

Tatiana grinned. "He made this one for me that same year, actually. Same design, just scaled down. Growing up, we had one my father had made from old metal hangers." Remembering the contraption that her mother had fondly dubbed "the metal monstrosity," she had to laugh. "It was horrible. Pabbi is good at many things, but making Christmas trees is not one of them. When Ari and Gunnar got married and my parents decided to give them the house and move to town, Mamma graciously offered to leave her the tree, and Ari graciously refused." She sent a wink to her niece.

It had been a very laughter-filled argument as each woman tried to escape Pabbi's dubious handiwork. That was when Gunnar had promised his bride a new tree.

He'd made one for his in-laws as well, and Mamma had given him a big kiss on the cheek in thanks while Pabbi pretended offense. There was no denying Gunnar's creation was superior in every way.

Still, part of her missed that rickety old wire version that had a tendency to fall apart if you looked at it wrong. It had been hideous, but it had made for good memories.

This one, however, had candleholders built in, and they were sturdy enough that she never feared them falling over and catching anything on fire. She pulled out the bundle of small white candles and handed them to Elea, who from her perch on the sofa had no trouble reaching even the higher branches. She passed a box of small glass ornaments to Anders and kept for herself the red ribbon bows to tie onto the end of each branch.

"We used to use candy as our ornaments," Anders said as he hung a shiny gold ball. "Which meant that when we took the tree down after Epiphany, we got to eat it. Our favorite day of the year."

Elea grinned. "Maybe when the war's over, we can do that. I love candy."

All the more, probably, because she got it so rarely these days. Sometimes it was strange to think that her niece had no memories of life in Iceland before the war. She'd been only a toddler when the British forces arrived, soon followed by the Americans. To her, this was normal—rationed food, American aircraft flying overhead every day, German U-boats interfering with their fishing.

She'd only know the richer Iceland that had come with the Americans. Which was good—Tatiana would be the first to say how glad she was that their economy had turned up so dramatically, given that it had allowed her to come to the city and chase her dream.

But she treasured all those memories of her own childhood. The ones built around finding ingenious ways to use every scrap, to create what they could never afford to buy. To read and tell stories because radios were too expensive, and small villages didn't have things like movie houses.

Anders made a show of sniffing one of the candles. "Oh, good. Not made from tallow. It would have been dangerous to put these out for Kertasnikir to steal otherwise. At the very least, you'd find some teeth marks in them tomorrow morning."

Elea made a face. "Who wants to eat *candles*?"

"Not spoiled little girls who have plenty of food to eat instead. But for a troll? Yum." Anders made as if to take a bite of one, which set Elea to giggling.

He'd be such a good father someday.

Tatiana's pulse hammered at the thought. Until a week

ago, she would have wondered with more than a tinge of jealousy what lucky woman would eventually overcome his bashfulness and convince him to propose. Now . . . it could be her. Maybe, if things went as she hoped they would, if he kept looking at her with his heart in his eyes . . . maybe *she'd* be the one who got to hold his heart. The one to walk through life by his side. Her children who could call him Pabbi.

She wanted it. She wanted it more than any present that could ever be put under a tree. Even though it had only been a week since they started down this path, even though he'd yet to even kiss her, she knew. He was the only man she'd ever met that she could imagine marrying. Spending the rest of her life with.

She'd been falling in love with him step by step, letter by letter this past year, after admiring him for years before that but deeming him unknowable.

Tying the last ribbon on the tree, Tatiana watched as Anders drew out her gold-painted star and gathered Elea in his arms so he could lift her to more easily reach the tip of the tree. Once she pushed it into place, they all clapped and cheered.

"Glethileg jol," Tatiana said. It truly felt like Christmas now, with juniper scenting the air and the star gleaming from the top of her little tree, with the lingering aroma of leaf bread and cookies coming from the kitchen, with her flat adorned and laughter filling it.

"Merry Christmas," Elea shouted in return.

Anders laughed and put her down, making a show of rubbing his ear. "I think all of Iceland heard you."

"Good! I wish them *all* a merry Christmas." She twirled around the center of the room and then grinned up at Tatiana. "Can I put my party dress on now? Can I? Can I?"

"All right." It was still awfully early, but why not? And while her niece dashed off and Anders settled with a contented sigh on her sofa, she decided she might as well make use of the opportunity. "So, tomorrow."

His face froze in that way it always did when he seemed to think bad news was coming. "You've decided not to come."

"No!" She laughed, shaking her head. Why did he always *do* that? "I am most definitely coming to your mother's. You can't rescind the invitation now."

His eyes went wide. "I wasn't—" At her next laugh, he sighed. "You know that."

"I do." She reached out and rested her hand on his wrist. "I was only going to say that . . . that I'd rather give you your gift beforehand, if that's all right. Or after. But . . . here, not there. So perhaps you could come a bit early to pick us up? Or you could plan to stay a bit after you bring us home again, after dinner."

"Or . . . both?" A single corner of his lips pulled up, hope—and a bit of daring—sparkling in his eyes.

A week ago, he wouldn't have dared to ask. She grinned. She'd eventually convince him to stop second-guessing this. Her. Them. But it could well take a while. Another week, at least. But perhaps, if all went well, by the time the calendar turned to 1945, he'd be ready to put more faith in them. "Both sounds perfect." Unable to resist, she reached out and ran her fingertips down the festive red tie he wore with his best gray suit. "Look at you, in something other than your usual blue tie."

"A nod to the occasion. Fair warning—I'll be wearing it again tomorrow. Unless I spill something on it tonight. In which case I'll have to hope it'll come clean and be dry by tomorrow, because if I show up to my mother's *not* wearing the tie she gave me last year, I'll never hear the end of it."

She smiled into his grin. "A mother's prerogative."

"I'd never say otherwise." He glanced down at her sturdy gray wool skirt. "I'm going to venture a guess that you haven't dressed for the party yet."

Her smile might have gone a little mischievous. "What? You don't think this is appropriate?"

He narrowed his eyes, cheeks only flushing a little. "The flour might at least need to be brushed off first. Though you look beautiful in anything."

She'd never been gladder that she'd splurged on a proper party dress last year, after Christmas, and had been saving it all this time. New clothes were a luxury she rarely indulged in—no one did, these days, with so much of the world's fabric going to the war effort. But the red gown in the secondhand shop had called her name, and it had been marked down, and . . . well, she had no regrets. "I'll go put my hair up and then change. I told Aunt Beta that we might come a bit early to lend a hand with any last-minute details, if we had the time."

"I'll entertain myself at your bookshelf."

Elea emerged from the bedroom as Tatiana was walking toward the bathroom. After giving a twirl in her own party dress—remade from one of Ari's old dresses, if she was identifying the fabric correctly—she dashed after Tatiana. "Can I have a crown braid for tonight?"

"Absolutely."

They pulled out the ribbons holding her usual two braids, loosened the strands, and then Tatiana got to work on the crown. Once finished, she shooed her niece out and set about pinning up her own hair, humming a carol as she worked.

She went ahead and applied her makeup too, pursing her red lips at the mirror and then smiling in satisfaction. Her dress was just this shade. Careful to keep her face pointed away from the main room as she emerged, she hurried into her bedroom and latched the door.

The dress had been waiting all year in a garment bag, which she unzipped now with a smile. It had long sleeves, slim and tapered at the wrist, but with gathers at the shoulder to give it just a bit of a puff. A neckline that went straight across from shoulder to shoulder, rouching along the left side from bust to waist, the lines it created running diagonally through the slender skirt. Simple, but elegant. And, she thought as she zipped herself into it and surveyed herself in the mirror, it fit like a glove.

Valdi threw this party every year, but she'd always gone home for Christmas . . . and sophisticated parties weren't exactly common in Hellnar. She'd never had cause to get so dressed up, but as she turned to try to see how the back was laying, she couldn't help but think she could get used to this tradition. It felt so festive. So fun.

And when she saw Anders's jaw drop the moment she stepped back out into the main room, she had to admit *that* was part of the allure too.

Idly, she wondered if he would have reacted like that had his first glimpse of her been at her uncle's, if this last week hadn't progressed as it had. Would he have turned from whoever he'd have been talking to like he now did from Elea and just stare at her as he was doing?

She hoped so. But didn't at all mind that there was no crowd of people between them. She pirouetted much like Elea had done earlier and struck a pose like one of the movie stars in the magazines. "Well? Better than my flour-dusted wool?"

For a moment, he just gaped, moving his mouth without saying anything. Then he smiled in that lopsided, uncertain way she loved. "Are you certain you want to go to this party with *me*? I can't fathom that I'm so lucky."

She grinned and moved closer. He held out a hand, and she put hers in it.

His eyes sparkled down at her. "You're gorgeous, Tatiana. I've never seen a more beautiful woman."

Not objectively true, but she could see he meant it. And if he really meant it, then surely it was because his feelings for her clouded his eyes. Oh, she hoped so.

He held out his arm. "Shall we?"

She tucked her hand into its new favorite place. "We definitely shall."

Elea ran ahead toward the door. "Let's hurry! I want to see the banana trees!"

TWELVE

24 DECEMBER 1944

Anders bent the last tack into place over the cardboard backing and spun the framed painting around, setting it back on the easel. He took a few steps backward, surveying his work critically.

Beside him, his mother tilted her head to the side. "Is it a bit skewed?"

"No. I measured four times." But was it? No. No, math didn't lie, but eyesight could, especially when affected by nerves. Case in point—though he'd been pleased with how the painting had turned out yesterday when he finished it before going out on the juniper hunt, just now he thought it the worst thing he'd ever done. "Do you think she'll like it?"

"If she doesn't, she's too much a fool for you to waste your time on." But Mother grinned and looped her arm around his. "It's beautiful, Anders."

His chest went warm and tight. He couldn't remember her ever saying such a thing about one of his paintings. Though, to be fair, he hadn't shown any to her, hadn't asked her opinion on them, in more than a decade. "Thank you for coming. Giving me your opinion on the frame."

He'd second- and third-guessed his decision to put it in one to match her other painting, not certain the stark black of that one would best set off the colors here. He'd needed someone else to weigh in.

His family hadn't been his immediate thought. Which was exactly why he'd called his mother. If he wanted things to change, he had to take the steps to make it so. Had to set aside all the years of hurt feelings and misunderstandings and try to grapple with the fact that he'd been wrong.

His family wasn't ashamed of him. His mother didn't hate the life he'd chosen. She didn't dismiss all his work.

She treasured it. Treasured it so highly she tucked it away where it couldn't be damaged. Where only she could see it, but see it every day.

Mother patted his arm. "Frankly, I was happy to escape the kitchen for a while. Kristin has it all in hand, anyway."

For the first time, he paused to wonder what it was like for his mother, living with Dalmar and Kristin and their boys. He'd always assumed she loved it, given that Dalmar was living the very life their family had always lived. The one she knew, was comfortable in.

But now he wondered if it was that simple. If perhaps after Father died, the house they'd raised their family in had begun to feel less hers and more Dalmar's. If she ever clashed with her daughter-in-law. If perhaps all the food she brought to Anders wasn't because she thought he couldn't take care of himself, but because she needed to feel useful. Needed to take care of *someone* . . . and Kristin *did* have a strong personality. She liked to be in charge. Perhaps Kristin, for her part, hated that the family still referred to it as Ommu's house, when it was hers and Dalmar's too.

Families were such complicated things. And he was going to do better being a part of his.

He leaned down and planted a kiss on his mother's cheek. "*Glethileg jol,* Mother."

She smiled up at him and, in a rare show of affection, reached up to pat his cheek. "She's the one, Anders. I know it. Knew it the moment I saw you walking together last week. And I . . . I couldn't be happier for you."

He held her gaze, returned her smile. "I'm so glad you like her. I still can't quite wrap my mind around the idea that she actually likes *me*, but . . . I don't intend to let her get away."

Mother turned toward the door, but her smile didn't fade. "I wish I could have seen you two last night at your fancy party. Did someone take photographs, at least?"

He nodded and moved with her. "Valdi's wife did, yes. She promised to get prints for everyone in the new year." A blink, and he was there again, in their festively decorated great room, an arm around Tatiana's back as she slipped one around his waist. The way they'd turned in together, then smiled for her aunt's camera.

It had felt so . . . real. Like they were really a couple. Truly together.

When the photographs came back, they'd probably show that he'd been mooning at her like a lovesick schoolboy, heart in his eyes.

That would be all right.

Mother tilted her head to the side as she stopped by the door, making her bun of silver and gold slip a bit. "Maybe next year I should impose a dress code on Christmas Eve. Tuxedos and evening gowns. What do you say?"

Laughter burst out. "Can you really imagine Ulric in a tuxedo?" His brother had grumbled about wearing a proper suit for his own wedding.

Mother's eyes danced. "No, but the look on his face if I were to suggest it would be priceless, don't you think? I'll tell him we need to bring some class to the place."

Still chuckling, Anders shook his head. "If you suggest it, I want to be there to see his reaction. But in truth, I don't want your Christmas Eve dinner to change." He was wearing the same suit and tie that he had last night, yes. But it would be an altogether different sort of party. No fancy music, no fancy food. His brothers—all but Ulric—would be in their Sunday best and his sisters-in-law would be in festive dresses, but there'd be no evening gowns or bubbling wine.

There'd be family. Laughter. They'd eat their meal of skate like they always did, and the exchange of gifts would be raucous and loud. He'd be the quiet one, sitting in his favorite chair, exchanging glances with Garri now and then as his nephew also retreated to a quiet corner with one of the books he'd receive. And this year, Tatiana would be at his side while Elea played with Heidi. Perhaps perched on the arm of that chair, or squeezed in beside him.

It would be perfect.

He reached for the coat his mother had hung on a hook when she'd come in and helped her into it. But to his surprise, she didn't then just say goodbye and reach for the door.

Instead, she turned to face him, her mouth serious now, laughter gone. "The other night, when Dalmar got home . . . he told me the advice you'd given him. About how he should behave with Garri."

Anders's shoulders went tight. "He never actually told me what he said—just that you and Kristin were angry with him for it."

Mother sighed. "It's so much easier to see, when I'm that half step removed. When *he* says something to upset his son, I can see the mistake in it. When it was me . . . when it was your father . . ." She shook her head, hands gripping the edges of the coat she'd yet to button. "We never meant to hurt you, Anders. Never meant to discourage. We just couldn't dream as big as you did. We didn't see how you could be anything but what we always were." A tremulous smile found her lips now, to match the tears he'd so rarely ever seen in her eyes. "Yet here you are! My baby boy, so successful. So wise that even *Dalmar* has to listen."

A laugh eked its way past his tight throat. "Did he?" He hadn't seen any of his brothers since that night, to hear what had happened after Dalmar got home.

Mother nodded. "When he got back, he went straight up to Garri's room. Kristin and I sneaked up to listen, afraid he would start shouting again. But he didn't. He apologized. And he asked to read Garri's story, said how proud he was. And then he even joked that Garri might have to explain any words he didn't know. Said later that one was yours, by the way."

Anders sagged against the door. "He really did listen."

His mother finally buttoned her coat. "You ought to have seen Garri the next morning. All but floated around the house, and his brothers had him read the story out loud to them five times since then." Her hands fell. "I'm sorry, Anders. Sorry we never did that for you. Sorry it took seeing my son hurt the feelings of my grandson over and again to realize I'd done the same to you." She held out a hand.

He took it, squeezed it. "I'm sorry too, Mother. I made so many assumptions over the years. Closed myself off, thinking . . . thinking you'd all be happier without me, I suppose. That you were ashamed of me."

She gripped his fingers so tight he would have yelped in exaggerated pain, had the conversation not been so serious. So good. "Never, Anders. *Never*. I was just . . . afraid. Afraid you'd outgrown us. That if I let you, you'd move on and forget all about us."

"Never." The hand wasn't enough. He pulled her into a tight hug, this woman who so rarely cried, who'd always seemed sturdy enough to weather any storm, who he'd never thought could bend or break. "I love you, Mother."

"I love you, my precious boy." She squeezed him tight, sniffed, and then pulled away to dash at her eyes, smiling. "Enough of this. You have a painting to wrap and a woman to woo. I'll see you at dinner."

He grinned. "See you at dinner."

Once he'd closed the door behind her, he strode to the easel and picked the painting up, lowering it carefully onto the paper he'd already laid out on the table. A few careful folds, a few lengths of tape, then all that was left was to tie the ribbon around it.

He cast a glance toward the pile of gifts he'd load in his car for his family—books, all of them—and wished once more that he'd had time to correct the mistake with Tandri. If Tatiana didn't like the painting, she'd still love the book, he knew.

Then he wished he'd had time to paint more, for his family. Scenes of whimsy for the children's rooms, perhaps some landscapes for his brothers and their wives.

Next year. There would be time enough to give everything on his heart, even if not today.

It took him several trips to get everything loaded into his car, careful to keep Tatiana's and Elea's gifts separate from the rest, so he could get to them first. At last he was driving the now-familiar route to her building, smiling through the swirling snowflakes.

It was Christmas Eve, the night they'd stay up to welcome

the celebration of their Savior's birth. A night known for the greatest miracle of all of history, when God lowered himself to become man—and here Anders was, living out a little sliver of his own miracle.

For the first time in his memory, he didn't feel *alone* on Christmas Eve. He felt . . . full. Surrounded. Loved.

He parked in front of her building, pulled out the two gifts, and was soon inside. He could hear Christmas music coming from a piano in a flat on the ground floor, families laughing together as he jogged up the stairs. He could smell the cooking skate that could no doubt be found in nearly every kitchen today. He reached her door and knocked. Drew in a deep breath.

Tatiana pulled it open, a smile already on her lips. She was wearing the red suit—the one he'd painted her in—and it made him smile too. That seemed like a good sign. "*Glethileg jol*, Anders."

"*Glethileg jol*, Tatiana." Catching sight of the little whirlwind spinning through the flat, he called out, "*Glethileg jol*, Elea." He held out the smaller of the packages. "I thought I'd better bring you something, in case Kertasnikir was so displeased that your candles weren't tasty tallow that he forgot to leave something in your shoe."

Elea slid to a halt in front of him, eyes wide as saucers. "You got me a present?"

He wiggled the box. "Certainly looks like it. Though I suppose it *could* be rotten potatoes, if you've been naughty."

Tatiana laughed as she snicked the door closed behind him. "I don't think Elea knows *how* to be naughty."

"Well, that's good. Because none of my potatoes were rotten." With a wink, he pushed the package into her little hands. "Go ahead."

The little one sent an excited look to her aunt and wasted no time moving to the table. She set the package down and peeled off the tape with care that made him laugh.

"Is this how you open presents? You're in for a shock at my family's house then. All those little monsters that I call nieces and nephews turn wrapping paper into confetti in about three seconds."

Elea sent him a horrified look. "They rip *this* paper? But you painted it!" She held it up in proof.

Tatiana gasped and pressed a hand to her mouth. "You *did*! Anders, why would you spend such time on *wrapping* paper?"

He grinned and shrugged, easing Tatiana's gift to the floor and leaning it against a table leg so he could take off his coat. "I started doing it when I was a child. It gets me in the Christmas spirit."

He'd never been entirely sure his family realized he still did it . . . but in retrospect, they *had* made a game of examining all the paper on all the gifts and taunting each other about whose was better. Could it be . . . was that their way of appreciating his work? Had his brothers' annual insistence that the cheapest paper to be found was the best just a tease?

Regardless, his nieces and nephews did indeed rip it to shreds. And he couldn't mind—that *was* what it was for.

Elea returned to her careful peeling of the tape, then eased the paper away. It meant she was greeted by the back of the gift rather than the front, so only once she'd flipped it over did her face light up. "Watercolor paints! And paper!" One item clutched in each hand, she rushed him and wrapped her arms around his waist. "Thank you!"

He chuckled and hugged her back. "You're very welcome. And I'll happily give you a few lessons before you go home, if you'd like."

"I would like, I would like!" She pulled away, spun to Tatiana. "Do I have enough time to draw something before we go? So he can show me how to paint it tomorrow?"

Tatiana smiled. "We still have half an hour. Go ahead."

He'd expected her to settle at the table, but instead, she dashed toward the bedroom and went so far as to close the door behind her, saying, "No peeking until I'm done!" as she closed it.

"I'm offended," he said. "She's let me look at her drawings every day as she works on them."

"I must be the one she doesn't want peeking." Tatiana clasped her hands, then unclasped them. She looked . . . nervous.

How odd—that was *his* role. But seeing it in her made him strangely relaxed. Enough, anyway, that he could reach for the wrapped painting without needing to wipe his palms dry on his trousers first. He held it out, met her gaze. "And for you."

The line of her shoulders softened, making him think her anxiety was about something else. "Come. Let's sit." She led him toward the sofa, and he smiled at the flickering candles on her tree, a bit surprised she'd lit them already.

He had a feeling Elea had made a plea she hadn't wanted to refuse.

Their dancing flames lent a festive air to the room, making him smile as he sank down beside her on the sofa.

Tatiana too took extraordinary care with the wrapping paper, despite his laugh. "Just rip it, Tatiana."

"I most certainly will not."

He shook his head. "What are you going to do, frame it and hang it on your wall? It's only wrapping paper."

"With the most adorable Yule Lads I've ever seen." Much like her niece, she peeled off the tape and folded the paper back, though the size of the painting meant she kept its bottom on the floor and leaned over it.

Once she had it loose, he helped remove the paper. She tipped the painting back, mouth in a perfect *O*. She blinked, gaze tracing over the image. Then she turned misty eyes and smiling lips to him. "Anders—it's . . . it's . . ."

He shrugged. "Jolabokaflod. Elea gave me the idea, and I couldn't help but create it."

"The Christmas Book Flood," she murmured, looking at the gift again. "It's perfect! Now I'll always have something to remember this year by." She traced a finger along the curve of painted-Elea's braid, though she didn't actually touch the glass. Then let the same finger run along the frame. "And it matches my other one! The frame, I mean."

"Mm. I debated. My mother talked me into keeping them a matching set."

"Your mother was right." She stood, moved the painting over to rest against the bookshelves on the opposite wall, and came back to the couch without taking her eyes from it, though she didn't sit. "Oh, wow. I needed a bit of distance to see all the details." She pressed her hands to her hips, looked down at herself, and laughed. "It's even this skirt suit."

"It seemed to fit the theme." Had he really been afraid she wouldn't like it? He smiled, watching her for several more moments as she took note of each detail, the titles on the spines of the books in her arms and on which Elea was standing—all ones she'd helped pack up and ship out these last few weeks. The books that were part of this first Christmas flood.

She pressed her hands to her cheeks. "I'll have to have Valdi and Beta over so he can see it. I wouldn't be surprised if he commissioned one from you too, to commemorate the Book Bulletin's success."

She and her niece clearly thought along the same lines. But Valdi wasn't his concern just now. "I'm glad you like it. I second-guessed myself about the painting too."

She spun to face him and gave him that look he was becoming so very familiar with. The one that was part chiding, part smiling, part . . . affection, he'd call it. He didn't dare give it any other name. Not yet. "Of course you did," she said. Then her face shifted, and she swallowed. Nodded. "That's your gift there on the table beside you. Under the tree—the one with green paper, which you really can just rip to shreds, because it's store-bought. The red ones are for Elea."

He thought he recognized the size and shape of one of Elea's and figured it for the signed copy of his latest saga that they'd chatted about before Elea ever arrived in the city. But he focused primarily on the green one. It was box shaped, the size of the boxes their typewriter paper arrived in—handy for gifts, to be sure. He'd repurposed several of them too.

Heavy, he noted as he picked it up. As heavy as if it really were just a ream of paper. And whatever was inside had Tatiana biting her lip in a way that made him nearly forget all about presents and lean in to show her how her lips ought to be treated.

Focus, Anders, he told himself. He tore the paper away, smiling at the familiar paper box, and sending a teasing smile her way. "Paper! You shouldn't have."

She finally sank back down to her place beside him on the couch. "You're not as wrong as your joke implies."

THIRTEEN

TATIANA BARELY KEPT HERSELF FROM gnawing all her lipstick from her lips as Anders lifted the lid from the box. Her stomach was in knots, scenarios nipping at her mind that she'd already entertained and dismissed a dozen times.

What if he couldn't reconcile Tatiana, the woman he admired, with Tandri, the author he thought he knew? What if the very idea of her being his newest author friend felt like a betrayal to him? For that matter, she didn't honestly know his opinion on female writers. True, he always treated the female employees at the Story Society with respect and equality, but they were all secretaries and assistants. Not editors. Not writers. The company had only a couple of those on the rosters, none of whom wrote stories like the ones she'd chosen to tell.

He set the lid aside, frowning a bit when he saw that it was, indeed, paper inside. A whole ream of it. But not blank paper—he'd be noticing the typewritten words covering it, behind the note sitting on top, on lined paper instead of blank.

He lifted the note. Frowned at the handwriting that would be familiar to him—not hers. Tandri Ebbisson's. She'd rewritten the thing so many times, she had it memorized.

Anders,

I couldn't sign that third book to myself—but it made me realize how very much I wanted you to know who "myself" really is. I wanted you to know me, the part of me I've yet to tell anyone else about. I wanted you—the man who first saw the worth in those words I'd penned anonymously, the man who helped me shape it into the book it needed to be . . . the man I've come to care for so deeply—to know the truth.

And that's all I can write in this hand, so put the note down now and look over at me.

Tatiana / Tandri

He obeyed, but his gaze flicked first to that typewritten page, where the title of her next book was written. *Beneath the Aurora*. The title of Tandri's second contracted novel.

His eyes went wide, but it wasn't disappointment or even shock that filled them. It was . . . did she dare to name it?

Her fingers twisted together. "Elea said I should give you a story I'd written," she said, words tumbling over themselves. "But I didn't have time to write something else, not with my deadline so soon—and I know this is a silly gift, because you can't actually *keep* those pages—I need to edit them. And then give them back to you, but as Tandri. To my editor. And . . ." She squeezed her eyes shut. "It's not even finished. I still have two chapters to write. But I wanted to give you something I'd never given to anyone else. Something true and meaningful and . . ."

"Tatiana." He reached out like she'd done over a week ago and caught her hand. "This is the best gift in the world. You've given me your trust. Your truth. Does no one else know?"

Could he possibly be as pleased as he sounded? As joyful? She shook her head in answer to his question.

"Your sister? Your parents?"

Another shake, and then a half-manic laugh. "Well, my lawyer, I suppose. He set everything up so I could sign contracts as Tandri. But he doesn't *know* me, so he doesn't count. But no one else. Not Valdi or Beta or Camilla, not my parents or Ari or Elea." Just him.

He squeezed her fingers, not asking why she'd kept her real name off the book. Why she'd told no one. He wouldn't need to. He, better than anyone, would understand the doubt, the fear, not to mention the bias she'd have faced.

He gave her a soft smile. "Elea was right. This is the perfect gift."

She let out a long breath, her uncertainty going out with the air. Then she drew in another, and let her lips curve up in that teasing way that always had his gaze dropping from her eyes to her mouth. "Well, I did have a backup plan for a gift. In case you didn't like the book."

He leaned a bit closer. "Did you? What was it?"

Her own pulse skittered as she said, "A kiss."

His smile only grew. "Well now I'm wishing I didn't love the book so much, so you'd have to resort to this backup plan."

"Mm. Or, since you received the first so graciously . . . perhaps you deserve a second." She scooted a little closer. Tilted her head.

His kiss was like the first flakes of snow drifting down, like the aurora dancing in the sky, like stars twinkling, like endless summer sunshine. It was light and music, color and wind, flowers and dreams. Tatiana let herself sink into it, her every sense abuzz. She let her hand lift to settle on his neck, scooted a little closer when his arm came around her.

She'd expected their first kiss to be tentative, shy, maybe even awkward. But it was none of that. It was slow and soft, but sure. Certain. Right. The kind of kiss that led to more kisses, years of them, a lifetime. The kind that said this moment was the first of forever.

It stretched out, long and languid as a winter night, and yet ended with the sweetness of spring. He drew in a deep breath, so she mirrored him. Looked into his clear blue eyes.

"Tatiana," he murmured, his lips still so close to hers that she could feel his breath as he spoke. "I've been in love with you so long. I never thought . . . and now I can think of nothing else. I love you. I need you to know that—I love you."

Her fingers curled into the ends of his hair. How had it all shifted so quickly? Gone from admiring him, savoring the few minutes she'd have in his company in a day, reading his letters over and over and wishing he knew they were to *her* . . . to this? "I thought I'd have to deny being in love with you for years yet—convince myself it wasn't that, couldn't be, because you'd never think of me like that."

She could feel his smile, see it in his eyes. "How could I think of anyone *but* you like that?"

She smiled back. "I'm glad you don't. Or rather, that you do. I love you, Anders."

He kissed her again, sending her senses swirling once more. But then the clock chimed its warning, and she put a few inches between them. One more thing still needed to be settled before they went to his mother's. "I have a favor to ask you."

The way he gazed at her made her think she could ask for the moon, and he'd find a way to harness it . . . or at least paint her the prettiest representation. "Anything."

She drew in a deep breath. "When it's time to take Elea home, would you consider driving us? I want you to meet my family. And more, I want you to be there when I give them their Christmas gifts."

He paused for a moment, clearly thinking it through. Then he grinned. "Signed copies of your book?"

She nodded. "It hadn't been my plan—I had other books for them already. But when I signed the ones for your mother and sister and you . . . I knew I wanted them to have them too. And I wanted them to know, even though it still terrifies me. What if they don't like it? What if *no one* likes it? It's sold well enough, yes, but I bet they've all been gifts, and no one's actually *read* it yet, and what if when they do—"

He pressed his lips to hers again, and she decided it was the nicest way anyone had ever told her to be quiet. "Your book, Tandriana"—they both smiled at the mash-up of her name and pen name—"will be well received because it's just that good. But even if your family doesn't like it, it doesn't matter. They'll still be so proud of you. They'll cherish those copies you give them, and they'll be bragging to everyone they know, if you let them."

She'd have to think about that part—whether she wanted anyone *but* her family to know that she was the one behind Tandri Ebbisson. A question for another day. One she could talk through with Anders—and oh, what a thrill it was to know she *could*.

He quirked a brow. "What about Valdi? Will you tell him?"

Though it required another deep breath, she nodded. "He deserves to know."

He nodded his approval. Then smiled. "My turn to ask for a favor."

Though she had no idea what it could be, she nodded. "Anything."

"After dinner tonight, after gifts have been exchanged with my family, may I come back here with you and Elea to read before midnight Mass?" He reached over and pulled the manuscript back into his lap, grin wide as a little boy's. "I can think of nothing I'd rather read tonight. But if I know authors at all, you don't actually mean to let me take it home quite yet."

Laughter tickled her throat. "I was going to let you—as long as you promised to bring it back tomorrow. But this is even better. Yes, that sounds like a perfect plan."

She and Elea had already decided that they'd exchange their gifts after they returned from Gilla's house, but she knew her niece wouldn't mind the addition. And then they could walk to church together, light their candles, sing of the most miraculous birth . . . she could think of no better way to celebrate their Savior. No better reminder of that truest Love that had ever been given, than to spend the hours counting down until his birth with the people she loved, reading other stories that could only hope to capture the most distant echo of his.

They shared one more soft kiss before it was time to blow out the candles on the tree and lure Elea away from her drawing with a reminder that Heidi was waiting for her. They all bundled up, Anders offered to carry the plate of cookies and leaf bread she'd prepared to add to the night's table, and soon they were in his car and trundling toward the harbor. She watched out the window with a smile as the streets took them closer to the home where he'd grown up.

The houses were closer together than in Hellnar, but otherwise this neighborhood wasn't so different from the place she'd always called home. And when they entered the house—all of their arms full of the packages Anders had prepared for his family—it felt familiar as well as new.

A house she'd never seen, but the comforting scents of home. Voices she'd never heard, but raised in shouts and laughter that could have come from her own family. Anders led her into the living room, Elea made a dash for Heidi, and three giants rose as one and made to devour them alive.

Anders, brave soul that he was, simply pointed to each in turn. "Dalmar, Ulric, Ram. I'd say they're nicer than they look, but . . ."

One of them tipped his head back in laughter, one lunged for Anders and rubbed his knuckles into his skull, and one bowed before her like some knight of old, saying, "We promised Mother we'd be on our best behavior for Anders's girl."

Gilla came in from another door, the smells of dinner accompanying her, and swatted the bowing son with the dish towel in her hands. "Always with the nonsense, Ram. Ulric, you're messing up your brother's hair. And Tatiana." Grinning wide, she flipped the towel onto her shoulder and reached out with both hands. Tatiana put hers into them. "Welcome. Our home is your home."

She gave those hands a squeeze, feeling the truth of the greeting. "Thank you, Gilla. What can I do to help?"

"Sit and be entertained." She pointed to a chair in the

corner. "Kristin won't let anyone else in the kitchen, but Garri's going to do a reading of his award-winning Christmas story."

"Is he?" Anders, having deposited all the presents somewhere or another, was smoothing his hair back into place. "Good. I've been dying to read it."

He'd told her about the story, about Dalmar burning fish and admitting his feelings, about the conversation they'd had. Last she'd heard, he'd gotten no update on how things had turned out, but this seemed like a good sign.

Especially when one of the brothers—Dalmar, she had to assume, given the gleam of pride in his eyes—nodded. "Prepare to be impressed, Anders. My boy's going to give you a run for your money when it comes to being the best writer in the family."

Yes, she could see herself with this boisterous group. She squeezed into the chair with Anders, exchanged hellos with the three women who soon skittered in from the kitchen and took up places beside their husbands, two snatching babies from the blankets where they'd been playing. The children who'd been racing in and out and around all elbowed their way into positions on the floor. And the eldest-looking boy took his place beside the real pine Christmas tree, wiped his hands on his trousers, took in a deep breath, and sent a quick look their way.

To Anders, she realized with a warm squeeze in her chest. Anders, who smiled at him and nodded, the arm he'd settled around Tatiana's shoulders giving a squeeze of its own.

Garri nodded back, looked all around at the gathered family, and let his gaze rest on his father, who grinned at him from the back wall. "The old witch, Gryla, hated Christmas," he began. "She refused to let it be celebrated in her home. But her thirteen sons always heard the songs drifting up from the villages, dancing into their cold gray caves, and they wondered. What was this day the people sang about? Who was this Jesus the people were celebrating? And so one year, they decided to find out . . ."

It was after nine by the time Tatiana unlocked the door to her flat and ushered Elea and Anders inside. Their arms were full again—this time with gifts she certainly hadn't expected to receive from the family who'd never even met her before today, aside from two of them.

But Ada had given her a novel that had been her favorite of the year; Kristin had presented her with a loaf of bread so beautiful Tatiana didn't know how she'd bring herself to cut it; Ram's wife had cheekily offered a small photograph of Anders in a frame that she could set on her desk at work, and Ulric's had kept the theme going with a photo album and a wink, saying she had a feeling there'd be many pictures to put in it soon.

Then Gilla had outdone them all. She'd given her a brooch. It was a simple wreath in brass, polished but clearly old. And said it had been her mother's. She'd given Tatiana, on their second meeting, when she and Anders hadn't even had an official date without a seven-year-old chaperone present, one of her family heirlooms.

Her feet hadn't touched the ground since, she was sure.

Elea dashed inside, deposited the handmade toys and books she'd gotten beside the table with the tree, and held up the box of matches. "Light it, Anders! Light the tree!"

"Let him get his coat off first," Tatiana chided on a laugh. He helped her from hers, too, and hung them both on the hooks. She rubbed a thumb over the brooch she'd already put on her lapel. When she looked up, she saw he was watching the motion, a soft smile on his lips. "You don't mind, do you? That she gave this to me?"

His smile went somehow gentler. "How could I?"

"Well . . . it's awfully official-seeming. And two weeks ago you could barely speak to me without clearing your throat three times."

He cleared it now, and then winked. "A lot can change in two weeks."

Praise God for that. She nodded toward the tree. "You'd better help with the candles before she decides to do it herself. I'll put some coffee on."

A few minutes later they were all settled in, and though she'd enjoyed her hours with his family, this was nice too—the quiet, the glow of candles, her little handmade tree. She sat beside Anders on her secondhand sofa and leaned into his side while Elea settled on the floor.

"All right," Tatiana said. "Go ahead and open them. But read the tags first—they're not all from me."

Elea's parents had sent one for her to open on Christmas Eve, as had both sets of grandparents. There would be a few more when she got home, Tatiana knew, but it was nice to have things to give her now too.

Elea tore into these without any of the care she'd shown Anders's wrapping paper, exclaiming with delight over the doll whose craftsmanship Tatiana recognized as her own mother's, the dress Ari had remade from another of her old ones, the notebook and pen from Gunnar's parents. Then she opened the newest volume of *Sagas for Children*, turned the page to see the signature, and leapt on the couch to give them both a hug.

Tatiana laughed and held her tight. "*Glethileg jol*, Elea. You've made this Christmas so happy for me."

"*Glethileg jol*, Aunt Tatta." She pressed a kiss to Tatiana's cheek. Then one to Anders's. "*Glethileg jol*, Anders." Then she pulled away with a grin. "Next Christmas, I want to call you *Uncle* Anders."

Tatiana gave her a playful swat. "Enough of your bright ideas. It's time to read."

"Not yet!" Elea dropped to her knees and reached a hand under the couch, coming out with a small, wrapped rectangle. "Your present, Aunt Tatta."

Tatiana took it, brows drawn. "When did you have time to do this?"

"Anders helped some," her niece admitted, plopping onto the couch on the other side of Tatiana.

Of course he did. She shot him a smile but then turned her attention to the gift. The paper was some of what she'd bought, so she tore it off. Then smiled in delight at the framed crayon drawing.

The second picture she'd received today of her and Elea, and she couldn't have said which one she loved more. "Oh, sweetheart. It's beautiful! Look at us—and even my typewriter!"

"Anders had to help with that."

Anders shook his head. "All I did was help you see it. *You* did the drawing."

Elea grinned. "Then he gave me the frame."

"Well, I love it. I'm going to keep it in my office at work so I can look at it any time I need a smile." She leaned over to kiss the top of her niece's head. "Thank you, Elea. I'll treasure it always." Then, just because she could, she leaned over the other way to press a soft kiss to Anders's lips. "Thank you, Anders, for helping her."

Elea giggled. "Told you he liked you."

Anders chuckled and reached for the sagas, passing the book over. "You've proven yourself to be very astute." His gaze moved to Tatiana. "What will you read tonight, *elskan min*?"

Her pulse fluttered at the endearment. He'd said he loved her, yes, but somehow hearing him call her "my love" made it even more real. "The novel your sister gave me, I think."

He plucked it from the pile of gifts and handed it to her. Then rubbed his hands together and reached for the manuscript in its box. "Come to me," he said, pitching his voice low and earning a giggle from Elea.

Tatiana's gaze moved over the pages in her book, but she couldn't have said what she was reading. She was too aware of the warmth of Anders's side, of every expression on his face as he read, of every typewritten page he flipped over into the top of the paper box. And she thought that maybe this wasn't such a brilliant idea. It had been bad enough when she'd known he was reading her first book at the office. But here? Beside him? When he knew it was hers?

"I can feel you fretting," he said as he flipped to the second chapter, a smile in his voice.

Tatiana puffed out a breath—and saw she was still on page three of her own book. "It's probably full of mistakes. I've edited those first chapters a bit, but—"

"Stop. It's good—just as I expected it to be."

She opened her mouth to object, but the phone rang. They all froze. Who would call this late on Christmas Eve? They'd already talked to Elea's parents earlier in the day, but she couldn't think of who else would be calling—not unless something was wrong.

She pushed herself up and dashed to the phone, telling herself not to worry even as her pulse pounded and her mind flew into frantic prayers. "Hello?" she said as soon as she had the earpiece in position.

"Tatta?" It was Gunnar's voice, and it sounded . . . anxious, excited? She couldn't quite tell. "Is Elea nearby?"

Excited. Definitely excited. That didn't calm her pulse any. "Of course. Elea." She waved a hand. "Your *pabbi* wants you."

"You stay on too, Tatta."

"All right." She dropped to her knees so that she and Elea could both put their ears to the receiver. "We're both here."

"*Glethileg jol* again, Pabbi!"

"*Glethileg jol*, precious. I have a special present for you."

"I just opened the dress Mamma made. It's so pretty!"

"I'll tell her you said so." His smile was audible. "But I have something even better."

Elea turned to meet Tatiana's gaze. "What is it?"

A beat, then a laugh. "A little brother! Your mamma just had your little brother, and they're both fine. Healthy, squalling—the baby, not your mother—and perfect."

Elea squealed so loudly Tatiana had to pull away with a laugh. But she could hardly blame her. They'd already had such a wonderful Christmas Eve—full of love and wonder and story. But this? There'd be no topping this. Though it would certainly make the night's scripture readings all the more poignant when they went to church. A new life, a son, a brother, to commemorate the Son of God, who had come to draw them all into his family.

Once Elea had quieted enough to allow for conversation, Tatiana put the phone back to her own ear. "I'm so glad, Gunnar. What will you name him?"

"Elias, after your father. When do you think you can get here with Elea? We miss her so much."

She smiled over at the little girl still dancing a jig in the center of her rug. At the man watching with a grin from his place on the couch, manuscript pages in his lap. He met her gaze, perhaps imagining what question had just been asked. Nodded.

"We'll be there tomorrow," she said into the phone. "Tell Ari to get as good a night's sleep as she can. We'll leave right after breakfast."

"Thank you, Tatta," Gunnar said, his voice sounding choked with emotion. "For keeping her. For making the holiday special for her when we couldn't."

Tatiana had to laugh. "Oh, trust me. She's the one who made it special." They said their farewells and she hung up, then went back to her place beside Anders and cuddled in.

It had been by far the best Christmas of her life. One of discovery, of love, of surprises, of truth. Of family, new and newly appreciated. She smiled and picked up her book.

All that, and it was just getting started. She could only imagine the joy tomorrow would bring.

About the Author

ROSEANNA M. WHITE is a bestselling, Christy Award–winning author who has long claimed that words are the air she breathes. When not writing fiction, she's homeschooling, editing, designing book covers, and pretending her house will clean itself. Roseanna is the author of a slew of historical novels that span several continents and thousands of years. Spies and war and mayhem always seem to find their way into her books . . . to offset her real life, which is blessedly ordinary. You can learn more about her and her stories at RoseannaMWhite.com.

A Note from the Author

WHEN I CONTEMPLATED WHAT SUBJECT matter to write about for a World War II novella, when my mind drifted over libraries and books as I was working on *The Collector of Burned Books*, a memory came to mind, of research I'd done into Jolabokaflod. In the bookish world, much ado is made over this Icelandic tradition of giving and reading books on Christmas Eve, and I knew that it began at the end of the war. The details, however, were harder to come by.

More research taught me that it began in 1944, and that the catalogue that was sent out to every household in Iceland—and which is still sent out annually today—was called the Book Bulletin. I learned that then, as now, every household purchased books. Then, as now, books were the primary gift that Christmas. I learned that every Icelandic publisher joined together to create and fund this Bulletin, and that it was a bigger success than they'd dreamed. I had to get creative on the details of how it worked logistically, as I couldn't find English-language descriptions of those details, but I hope my depiction of both the joy and the overwhelm aren't too far off.

As I researched this tradition, I learned that Iceland is a nation of storytellers. From their epic poems to their sagas to the stories they tell around their dinner tables, the people of this small island nation are considered some of the most avid booklovers in the world, far outpacing any other country in the percentage of people who read for fun.

I was also fascinated to learn that Iceland had been occupied during World War II, not by Nazis like the rest of Scandinavia, but by the Allies. And I was even more fascinated to learn that they call it "the blessed war." Unlike so many other nations, Iceland boomed thanks to American dollars and American export opportunities, taking the people from the poorest to among the richest in Europe in a few short years. Icelanders were very wary of their occupiers, though, with the older generation forbidding the younger one, especially young women, from fraternizing with their occupiers, resulting in very little interaction (though of course there was still some).

And learning about Icelandic society and traditions was just as interesting! I loved the tradition of the Yule Lads, which they use in their Christmas celebrations instead of St. Nicholas or Santa Claus, and had to find a way to bring them into the story. That was what inspired the novella you now hold—not just the origin of Jolabokaflod, but the quest to bring joy to one little girl, who in turn brought joy to those around her, through the tales of the mischievous Christmas Trolls.

A quick note on Icelandic naming traditions—even to this day, Icelanders do not have surnames like we know them. Instead, each child is named after their father. So Anders, son of Johann, is Anders Johannsson (literally "son of Johann"), as are his brothers, while his sister is Ada Johanndottir ("daughter of Johann"). Thanks to this long-standing naming tradition, there's no equivalent of our "Mr. Johannsson" or "Miss Eliasdottir" in their society. They simply call each other by their first names. Having been so accustomed to the more formal address of other European countries in historical times, this took some getting used to!

It's also interesting to note for word nerds like me that while Icelandic uses the Latinate-based alphabet, as we do in English, they omit several letters that we use (*C*, *Q*, *W*, and *Z*) and have several letters we do not, namely *Ð/ð* (eth), *Þ/þ* (thorn), *Æ*, and *Ö*. While the two vowels are more familiar to English speakers and denote sounds that are variations we recognize, the two consonants are both variations of the *th* sound—*ð* makes the *th* sound like in *breathe*, while *þ* makes the *th* sound of *breath*. Though our English-reading eyes look at them and see a *d* and a *p*, the sounds are very different. For ease of reading, we decided to spell things phonetically for English readers, leaving out those letters we don't have, as well as the many accents that are in actual Icelandic.

I hope you enjoyed this peek into what the first Jolabokaflod, the Christmas Book Flood, might have meant for a few book-loving families . . . and that it's perhaps inspired you to make this Icelandic tradition part of yours!

Three-quarters of my family embrace it wholeheartedly, staying up long into the night on Christmas Eve to read our new books . . . while my son rolls his eyes at us and opts for video games instead. But even he loves to tell stories. They're part of our family, and I pray that this one that brought me such delight as I wrote it helped you pass a few happy hours too.

May your Christmas be merry, bright, and filled with good stories! *Glethileg jol!*